Chapter One

The woman in front of him ducked into an alley, and it was everything Luke Jackson could do not to curse. If he didn't have this blasted bum leg, he'd have had no problem keeping up with her—or remaining undetected. Another glance at the photo his ex–squad mate Flannery sent him three days ago, and he gritted his teeth and picked up his pace. Every stride sent a dull pain from his knee. It had been replaced almost two years ago after being shot out on what was supposed to be a routine search-and-rescue. The doc said he'd made a startling recovery. She'd called him a miracle. He sure as hell didn't feel like a miracle when they were serving him his walking papers.

But there was no use thinking about what he lost.

He was here to keep Ryan Flannery's idiot childhood friend safe. She was the reason he'd been camping out in Cork and ghosting around Blarney Castle for the last forty-eight hours. Her sister was sure that she'd go here first, so this was where he'd shown up to pick up the trail.

What kind of woman just up and left her life behind to backpack through Europe alone?

Obviously not a smart one.

It was because of her impulsive decision to take off with only a text message as good-bye that he'd been sitting in the rain for so goddamn long, he was in danger of never getting warm again. It was worse in a way, because it'd just been a fine mist all day, rather than a torrential downpour that would make it easier to justify staying indoors. If he and Flannery hadn't been in the PJs together and fought their way through hell and back more times than he could count, he wouldn't be in this goddamn country, camped out because he couldn't guarantee that this woman wouldn't make an appearance.

Sure enough, she'd waltzed up around lunchtime, and now here they were.

He reached the alley entrance. With his luck, the woman was going to get jumped before he could catch her. He hadn't expected her to hike back to Cork from Blarney Castle, and he hadn't been able to risk a cab for fear that she'd get into trouble while he wasn't watching her.

He never should have agreed to this favor.

Luke turned the corner—and got kicked in the face.

He hit the wall hard enough to bruise, and barely got his hands up in time to deflect the next blow. He managed to block her next few punches, his body going through the motions like it had a thousand times before. He glimpsed a flash of hazel eyes and a determined expression, and then Alexis Yeung zeroed in on his damaged knee. Pain exploded behind his eyelids, but even that wouldn't have normally slowed him down. No, it was the damn knee giving out and sending him tumbling to the ground that did him in.

Luke rolled onto his back just in time to catch sight of a can that looked suspiciously like pepper spray. *Fuck that.* "What the hell?" He lurched up and grabbed her wrist, shoving her arm wide so the spray hit the ground next to him instead of his face.

"Why are you following me?" She tried to jerk away, but he wasn't letting her go anywhere until he had control of the canister.

He squeezed the pressure point in her wrist and snatched the can as it fell from her hand. It was only then that he registered her question. "What?"

"Why are you following me?" She scrambled back a few steps, but her voice was low and calm despite the circumstances. "You know what? Don't bother answering that. I'm calling the police."

Shit. That was the last thing he needed. As he climbed to his feet, Luke searched for something to say that would make her pause enough to listen to reason. He couldn't tell her the truth—Flannery had been pretty damn clear on that. If she knew her friends and sister back home didn't trust her, Alexis would never forgive any of them. Which sounded pretty damn juvenile, but it was the least of his concerns right now. If she called the Garda, he would have no choice but to come clean. "What are you talking about?"

"You've been following me ever since I left the castle. I might be a tourist, but I'm not stupid."

If he didn't have a bum knee, she never would have known he was there. The failure burned his throat almost worse than the pepper spray would have. "You're crazy. It was a nice day so I wanted to walk."

"Even with that limp? In the rain?"

Well, hell. She'd noticed a lot more than he would have given her credit for, even with his staying well back on the road. "I'm not a cripple." Though when he compared his limits now to what they'd been before his injury, he sure as hell felt like one. He scrubbed a hand over his face. "And you obviously thought it was a nice enough day for a walk in the rain. Pot, meet kettle."

She paused, clearly taking him in. Alexis Yeung, nurse and apparently sufferer of a mental breakdown when her perfect life didn't go exactly as planned. Really, she was just throwing a temper tantrum by jetting off to Europe to find herself or whatever it was that high-maintenance women did.

She didn't look like much. Oh, sure, she was beautiful in a very busty Asian-babes way, but what kind of woman spent the day hiking down a road and managed to look so perfectly put together? It wasn't natural. Her jeans were rolled up to show off her hiking boots, and her white T-shirt didn't have a smudge of dirt on it. He tried not to notice how the fabric strained over her breasts, and failed.

"Stop staring at my chest."

"Woman, you just attacked me for no reason. The *least* I deserve is to check you out." She crossed her arms under breasts, and he raised his eyebrows. "You're not exactly helping my concentration, darlin'."

"You're a pig." The woman had a stare on her that made him think of his auntie. He shoved the comparison away. Aunt Rose wasn't anything like Alexis. She didn't run from her problems—or other people's problems, for that matter—not even when they were literally knocking on her door. This woman obviously did, or he wouldn't be in a back alley in Cork getting grilled.

Alexis looked like she wanted to kick him again. "Why did you turn down the alley?"

This, at least, he had an answer for. "You're a woman alone. I thought you might be in danger."

"So you came riding to my rescue on your white horse?" And now she was laughing at him.

He coughed, hating the slow heat of embarrassment working its way through him. *He* wasn't the one in the wrong here. "Only an idiot wanders down a dark alley alone."

"I'm more than capable of taking care of myself."

A fact Flannery had left out in his description of her, which made Luke wonder what else he'd left out. "Against a man with a bum leg." Which hurt like a bitch after the combination of the hike and the beating she'd given it.

"Whatever you have to tell yourself to sleep at night." She paused. "Give me back my pepper spray."

"Not a chance." There was nothing to guarantee she wouldn't try to spray him again, and he'd suffered through enough shit today.

"It's mine."

"Yeah, well, you lost the right to it when you attacked me." He sounded like a grumpy old man, but her very presence pushed buttons he didn't know he had.

No, that was a goddamn lie. He knew every single one. Hell, he was more button than man these days.

She glared. "I'm leaving now. If you try to follow me again, we'll go another round and I'll come out on top. Again."

If there wasn't the slightest wavering in her voice, he might actually believe she was an international badass like she seemed to think. Then again, if this little slip of nothing could get the drop on him, then he'd fallen even further than he could have guessed. Humiliation tore through him, demanding he win back some of his damaged pride. "Darlin', you got the drop on me once. It wouldn't happen again."

"Right. Because you're not following me."

"Nope." Though he kind of wanted to douse her in cold water for how smug she sounded. Luke shrugged out of his pack. He heard more than saw her tense. "Relax, Rambo. I'm just tucking this away for now for safekeeping." He shoved the pepper spray into his pack, needing to do something to keep her from taking off. He didn't know how much more jaunting around he could take today. Add in the bonus of not knowing where the hell she was staying—or where she was going next—and he had to do something drastic. "The least you can do is buy me a drink after attacking me."

"Attacking you? That's rich. Maybe you shouldn't be creeping into alleys after lone women. When you're acting like a predator, expect to be treated like one."

She had a point, which only served to annoy him more. Luke shifted and tried to hold back a wince when his knee protested. "Buy me a drink and we'll call it even." At least that would give her crazy ass a reason to sit still for a little while. If he could get her talking, maybe he could figure out her next step to self-discovery or whatever the hell she was trying to accomplish over here in Europe. Her sister and Flannery hadn't been the least bit helpful on that note.

"That's funny. You should be a comedian." She shook her head. "If anything, *you* should buy *me* a drink for scaring me half to death."

It was a seriously perverse joy to throw her own words back into her face. "You can take care of yourself."

She threw up her hands. "Forget this. You're obviously not suffering from any issues besides being an ass. Have a nice life."

Damn it. He'd let his mouth get away with him—again—and fucked this all up. Luke limped after her. "Hey."

Alexis paused at the mouth of the alley. "You reconsider that drink?"

He didn't want to. Buying her a drink was all but admitting that she was right. But his pride couldn't hold up to the throbbing in his knee. He took a deep breath and tried to wrestle down his anger. It wasn't completely her fault. If he weren't damaged goods, they wouldn't be in this position to begin with. "First round's on me."

Alexis Yeung wasn't sure whether to be proud of herself or feel bad for taking out some stranger who apparently was only following her to save her from some imagined bad guy. It was almost enough to make her feel guilty for attacking him, especially when he was blatantly trying not to favor his knee because of the hit she'd gotten in. *Great job, Alexis. The guy is trying to be a Good Samaritan and you knock him on his ass.*

But every time he opened his mouth, the guilt threatening dissolved a bit more. This guy was no different from the ones back home—totally sure he knew better than the helpless little woman that she was. He was just like her ex-fiancé

Eric—the kind of man whose masculinity revolved around being the strongest, smartest, best person in the room. Anyone who threatened that was taken down a few notches with pointed comments and, if that failed, all-out bullying.

She pegged this particular man as one who skipped the rest of the steps and jumped straight to being a bully.

It would be smart to tell him where to stick his crappy attitude, and head back to the hostel to shower and search out food in a less hostile environment, but she was tired and hungry, and passing up a free drink would be silly. Plus, she was capable of spending a little more time with this guy, if only to assure herself that she really *was* growing and stronger than she'd been when she left Wellingford. That was the whole point of this journey she'd started, and she wasn't going to be doing any emotional growing while hiding in her hostel room.

She'd lived her entire life by the rules. Now it was time to take chances—just not stupid ones. She watched him out of the corner of her eye. Her one kick alone wouldn't cause him lasting harm. *If he turns out to be a creep, I can outrun him with no problem. Or take out that knee again, and* then *run.*

Satisfied she wasn't making a stupid decision in the name of being strong, she said, "There's a little pub down this street. Sin É."

"I know it."

Of course he did. She bet he just knew everything. How a Southern boy—and there was no mistaking *that* accent—knew his way around Cork was a mystery. Even if he was a world traveler, he seemed more the type to immerse himself in Dublin's frenetic energy and partying than the slightly calmer western half of the country. Then again, it was Ireland. Drinking was practically the national pastime. This guy probably fit right in.

Which reminded her—she had no idea what his name was. Alexis turned around as they stepped back onto the street and nearly gasped out loud. She'd caught glimpses of him on the road back from Blarney Castle, but they'd been just enough to place the tall, lumbering blond who seemed to cart around a chip on his shoulder. And then, when he'd come around the corner of the alley, she'd been more concerned with fighting for her life than checking him out.

Now…now, she was forced to admit that he was attractive in a rumpled, roguish sort of way. His shaggy blond hair and almost-beard made him look like he'd be more at home wearing flannel and chopping wood than globe-trotting, but who was she to judge? She almost laughed. Who was she kidding? She was judging the hell out of him. He wore faded jeans and boots that looked like they'd seen some use. Against her better judgment, she lifted her gaze to the black T-shirt hugging his shoulders and biceps, highlighting the tattoos crawling down his arms. Only one side was finished, though, but he moved before she could pinpoint exactly what the tattoos depicted.

"Why don't you whip out your smartphone and take a picture? It'll last longer."

She didn't bother to correct him. Alexis had very specifically left her cell back in Pennsylvania when she left. She didn't want her sister, Avery, or any of their friends to have a way to track her down. This trip was something she had to do for herself, and that meant stepping away from her pregnant sister and the overprotective Flannery brothers.

They'd only become more protective since Avery and Drew got engaged. She wasn't anywhere near as close to them as her sister, but they were still like stand-in older brothers when it suited them. She had a feeling it would suit them just fine in this situation. It had been annoying when she was a teenager. Now, with Ryan an experienced pararescuer and Drew the town sheriff... Yeah, it had passed beyond annoying and into the downright ridiculous. The fallout when she got home was going to be a nightmare, but maybe then she'd finally feel centered enough to deal with it.

In the meantime, she had this guy to deal with. "What's your name?"

He hesitated, and she wondered if maybe he'd tell her to screw off. Getting a drink with him wasn't mandatory by any means, but she refused to do it while considering him "that guy" in her head. Finally, he sighed as if resigning himself to something—probably her company for however long it took to down a drink. "Luke. My name is Luke."

It seemed too clean-cut a name for him. He looked like someone who would be called Jake, or Murphy, or Adonis. She bit her lip. No, not Adonis. He was attractive, but he wasn't *that* attractive.

Sure. Just keep telling yourself that.

"I'm Alexis." Then, before she could talk herself out of it, she turned left toward the corner where she could already hear strains of a jaunty fiddle coming out of the pub.

Chapter Two

Alexis could feel him at her back all the way down the street and through the pub door, and she wasn't a fan of how crowded the bar suddenly seemed as soon as Luke followed her in. He wasn't one of those massive meatheads, but he took up more than his fair share of space. He wasn't touching her, but his presence made it hard to draw a full breath.

Probably because he was such a pushy ass.

As if her thinking it was his cue, he shouldered past her and led the way to two stools tucked into the back corner of the bar. She spared a look around as she followed, taking in the Christmas lights strung across the ceiling and the band huddled around a tiny table, playing music and singing in such thick accents, she could barely understand the words. But, God, it was beautiful music. It simultaneously tore at her heart and made her toe want to tap in time. She spared them a smile as she took the seat beside Luke.

He glowered at everyone, and even the grizzled old bartender seemed hesitant to approach. Alexis sighed, already regretting agreeing to this drink. She was going to end up stuck here for hours because he was scaring off the locals. "Hey, you, tone down the He-Man menace."

"He-Man was the good guy."

She eyed him. It just figured that he'd know that. *He's probably a Superman fan, too, if the hero complex that made him chase me into an alley is anything to go by.* "That doesn't make him less scary to your average joe—and if you don't knock off the bitch face, we're never going to get drinks."

He blinked, drawing her attention to the fact she could actually tell his eye color now. It aggravated her for absolutely no reason that they weren't anything as mundane as blue or brown or even her own hazel. No, this ass had a green so light, it could almost be termed sea-green. Luke's brows dropped, which didn't do a single thing to help his angry expression. "What the hell is 'bitch face'?"

"You should know. It seems to be your permanent expression." And what did he have to be so angry about? They were in a beautiful city, rich with history and lore and a thousand other things. She'd been here only two days and she already felt a little lighter on her feet—something she would have thought impossible even a month ago.

Except she *had* just kicked the hell out of his knee. If it was as she suspected, and he had an old injury there, that would certainly explain some of the nasty attitude he was throwing her way.

That, and the fact that he'd shown up to save her, and she hadn't needed saving in the first place. Something like that would piss off her ex something fierce. She glanced down at the bar. *Damn it, I came here to move into the future, not dredge up the past.* "Have you ever tried being nice to people?

"We can't all be dancing through the tulips and breaking into song with whatever animal happens to be closest."

Alexis blinked. "Did you just compare me to a Disney princess?"

His grin shouldn't have sent a spark through her, but she rationalized that it was anger making her perk up—not anything so stupid as desire. Luke propped his elbow on the bar and leaned against it. "If the glass slipper fits."

He looked so incredibly smug, she wanted to grab the nearest drink and throw it in his face. He really thought he had her number. She wasn't sure why she was surprised. Sometimes it seemed like everyone she came into contact with, from her judgmental grandparents all the way down to the waitress at her favorite diner back home, thought they knew all there was to know about her. Why would this man be any different? "You don't know a damn thing about me."

"I know enough." Luke's gaze raked over her, seeming to take her in and dismiss her in one smooth move. She hated him for it. People had been doing the same thing for most of her life—looking at her for what she could bring to the table, or what she could do for *them*. All found her disappointing. They never cared enough to look beyond the surface.

"What are you running from, princess?"

Everything.

But she didn't have to come halfway across the world to cry her heart out to some man who no doubt couldn't care less. She wasn't looking to be saved, or for outside fulfillment. She wanted to get right inside her own head.

He wouldn't understand that, though, and it was

definitely too deep for bar talk. "I'm here to be a tourist. Same as anyone else."

He snorted. "Whatever you have to tell yourself."

Good God, the man was pricklier than a cactus. She was already tired of being on the pointed end of his questions—especially when every answer she gave was met with a response like *that*. "What about you? You don't strike me as the type to enjoy historical monuments."

"Now who's throwing stones?" The bartender finally got up the courage to approach, and Luke ordered two beers without even asking her. Before she could correct him, the man was gone. *High-handed much?*

Luke turned his attention back on her. "Maybe I went up to kiss the Blarney Stone."

Her gaze dropped to his mouth. She could almost imagine those wickedly curved lips pressing against the cool stone…and other things. His mouth twitched up, and she jumped. Crap, had she really just been checking him out? And worse, he'd caught her. Alexis tried to push down her ridiculous reaction. "If you did, the gift of gab didn't take."

"So quick to kick me while I'm down." His tone dropped a full octave and took on a downright sinful edge. The anger didn't go away, exactly, but it focused in on her like a laser. "It makes a man think unforgivable thoughts."

She couldn't get over how… Alexis had a hard time putting it into words. How *male* he was. He took up that stool like he owned it, as if he'd never been unsure of his place in the world. And that accent—she'd bet he could charm the birds from the trees if he got that stick out of his ass long enough to do it. But she couldn't afford to forget just how little he obviously thought of her. Strange attraction or not, she wasn't going to touch him with a ten-foot pole. "Do they involve a hacksaw and a pig farm?"

That was what she thought of him? A goddamn serial killer? Luke growled. So maybe he deserved the judgment, but that didn't make it stick in his throat any less. He'd been an ass and he damn well knew it, but there was something about Alexis that got under his skin—like an itch he couldn't reach. "That's rich coming from a woman who goes around attacking innocent bystanders."

"Oh, please. There's nothing innocent about you, and we both know it."

Yeah, he did. He wouldn't be over here in Ireland in the first place if he didn't have ulterior motives. The fact that they weren't *his* ulterior motives didn't change a damn thing. He owed Flannery his life a couple times over. A man didn't forget a debt like that. So when Flannery called, Luke didn't hesitate to drop everything and hop the first plane over here, no questions asked.

Last time he was in Wellingford, Luke had met Alexis's sister, Avery. The sisters shared some superficial similarities—both Chinese and beautiful—but it ended there. Avery might be brash, but she didn't have the ability to hit below the belt like Alexis did. And Alexis...she looked like she'd wandered out of a fairy tale, yet there was none of the inherent sweetness of those princesses he compared her to. But when push came to shove, she'd seen as little of the horrors of life as they had. It must be nice to sit on her golden throne and look down her nose at broken men like him.

And yet… He wanted her.

Luke paid the bartender and took a long pull of his beer while he dealt with *that* unwelcome realization. He hadn't had the time for or interest in women since his nearly full recovery from the IED hit. No, that wasn't the truth. He'd tried, that single time, with the woman he met at his local watering hole. Anger and shame burned through him all over again as he remembered the disgusted look on her face right before she hightailed it out of his room.

It would be his shitty luck that his cock would perk up in the presence of this haughty woman who didn't hesitate to hit him where it hurt—physically and otherwise. He couldn't deny that she was gorgeous, with her long black hair and her body that just wouldn't stop. But then she opened her mouth and shot it all to hell.

"Stop looking at me like that."

He should back off. Poking at her was just going to make the animosity between them grow, and he was supposed to be keeping track of her until she got the bug out of her ass and went back stateside. Until then, like it or not, they were stuck with each other—even if she didn't know it.

Considering the runaround she'd given him over the last few days, he'd have to be a damn fool to complicate things further. Even if she were interested, she'd react the same way the last mistake had. Pretty princesses were looking for knights in shining armor to ride out and save them from their problems.

He was a battle-scarred old wolf, far more likely to eat her whole than give her the sweet kind of sex she craved. But he couldn't stop himself from leaning a little closer and crowding her. "Like what?"

"Like you're about to start a brawl or..." She hesitated, licking her lips. There was definite interest sparking in those hazel eyes. So the princess liked to play on the dark side? She wasn't stupid—in the middle of some kind of quarter-life crisis, sure, but not dumb. She knew he couldn't give her the sunshine and rainbows that another man could.

Let it go. He couldn't. "Or?"

Another swipe of her tongue over those pale pink lips that he'd been doing his damnedest not to stare at since she sat down next to him. Alexis looked away, seemed to gather herself, and met his eyes. "Or drag some woman out of here by her hair."

Just like that, he could picture hauling her ass out of here. Not by her hair, no. He wasn't that much of a savage. But it was all too easy to imagine dragging her behind him and pinning her against the nearest wall to teach that mouth of hers some manners.

Christ, he was in serious trouble. He'd bet the last thing Flannery had intended when he called Luke was for him to get into a compromising position with Alexis. But the brakes were gone, and he was dangerously close to losing control. "Who said I'm not planning on doing just that?"

She raised her eyebrows. "Well, it'd certainly be in character, wouldn't it? You're not exactly a bundle of surprises at this point."

This woman had taken one look at him and acted as judge, jury, and executioner. It made him twitch, though hell if he could decide if he wanted to toss her out on her ass or kiss her until she got off her high horse—or just got off. Thoughts he couldn't afford to be thinking, especially about her, but Luke couldn't let it rest. There was something about this woman that scraped at his control, and he'd be damned before he let her get the last word. "Says the woman who's one giant cliché after another."

"Excuse me?"

"Look at you." He waved a hand in her direction and somehow managed not to focus on her breasts again. "You have no connection to reality. I bet you just woke up one day and thought it'd be a lovely idea to jaunt halfway across the world and see some of Europe."

"I had my reasons."

Warning bells went off in his head, but he was too far gone to shut up now. "So you're running from something—in the most cliché way possible. What, did you read *Eat, Pray, Love* and figure that if it worked for her, it'd work for you, too?"

Alexis's mouth went tight. "Please. You should listen to that old saying about throwing stones from glass houses. You have 'runner' written all over you." Her eyes dropped to his knee and then rose to his face. "Though I doubt you could outrun a turtle at this point."

He wanted to shake her until some degree of sense popped into that gorgeous head of hers. His injury had been life-ending, even if he'd kept right on breathing through the worst of it. There were days, dark days he didn't like to think about, where he wondered if maybe it was all a mistake. If whatever passed for a God in this world had lost interest for the few seconds it took for the doctors to pull him back from the edge and patch him up. Aunt Rose would whup his ass to know he thought like that, so he didn't tell her. He didn't tell anyone.

But he sure as hell wasn't going to open up about *that* to this woman who seemed to like taking him out at the knees. "I fucked up my knee saving a man's life. Running marathons might not be in my future, but he gets to go home to his family because I was there." *Saved the patient, but let my brother-in-arms die. A great fucking legacy to have.* Not that he was going to tell her that. She didn't deserve a window into the private pain he lived with.

Luke braced himself for the sympathy or, worse, pity that he got when he told the abbreviated version of how he got hurt. But she surprised him. "Heroic thing to do." She raised her eyebrows. "But if you're at peace about it, then why the hell do you stomp around, dragging your knuckles and glaring at everyone? No, I don't think so. Luke, I do believe your nose is growing by the second."

Voices raised on the other side of Alexis, two burly men shouting about… He couldn't quite catch it. But the writing was on the wall when the taller of the two shoved the other. *Shit.* Luke moved as the short man shoved back, hauling Alexis into his lap and getting an arm up in time to deflect the man's fall. By that point, several other guys got involved, dragging the original two outside. A heartbeat passed, and another, and then the musicians started up again, a slow, haunting melody that raised the small hairs on the back of his neck.

He started to breathe a sigh of relief that the situation hadn't gotten truly out of control, when she shifted and he realized that they were seriously up close and personal. Her dark hair was tousled, and her chest rose and fell with each harsh breath. He stared, knowing he should say something or do something to break the tension building between them, but all Luke could see was the way her lips parted as if in invitation.

Goddamn it.

Chapter Three

Luke was going to kiss her. Alexis could read it on his face. Now was her opportunity to laugh again, slide off his lap, and retreat to her own stool. She hadn't meant to be so harsh with him, but her lack of control these days was part of what spurred her to take this trip in the first place.

Her inability to say the right thing was part of the reason she'd started her journey here in Cork with visiting the Blarney Stone. Her mother used to regale both Alexis and Avery with stories of Ireland and the faerie folk and all the magical things that happened on the green isle. She wasn't a child anymore, and her mother was dead and gone, but the magic of those stories still held a special place in Alexis's heart.

Her life had become so dull and heartbreaking that every day seemed to sink her deeper into a mud pit of depression she couldn't escape. So she'd come here, to arguably one of the most magical places on earth, to begin to wash the muck away. To learn to love her life again, the way her mother had loved life…even when death was knocking at her doorstep.

And now here she was in a situation that never would have come about at home, sitting on the lap of a man who was barely more than a stranger and considering kissing him—considering doing a whole lot more than kissing him if she was honest.

There was something about this painfully attractive, brooding man that set her teeth on edge and made her restless, all at the same time. She hadn't pulled her punches, and he certainly wasn't holding back for fear of hurting *her* feelings. He was the first person she'd come across in a long time who didn't dance around her for fear of saying something that would hurt her. It was as refreshing as it was aggravating. The barb about *Eat, Pray, Love* hit entirely too close to home. She'd read that book just last month, and it had felt like such a profound step in her journey to take control back in her life.

None of that seemed to matter now, not when he watched her as if she were the most important thing in the room, as if he were losing his mind just being this close to her. Before she could talk herself out of it, Alexis tipped her face up, inviting him to follow through on the promise in his pale green eyes.

Kiss me, please kiss me, and make me forget all about the countless things trying to drag me under.

Luke froze, and for one eternal second she thought she'd misread his signals. But then his mouth crashed down on hers, erasing any chance of misinterpretation. His tongue speared between her lips, stroking along her tongue once, twice, a third time. She couldn't fight back a moan as he raked his teeth over her bottom lip before sucking it into his mouth. The spark of attraction inside her burst into an all-out bonfire. Alexis shifted her grip, letting go of his shirt with one hand so she could twine her fingers through his longish blond hair. She pulled it sharply enough to make him groan against her mouth, and then he was kissing his way along her jaw and nipping her earlobe. "You taste so goddamn good, darlin', like a Georgia peach. I can't get enough of it."

Thank God, because if he stopped right now, she might not recover. She'd never felt such all-encompassing need pounding through her veins, pushing her to do something she'd never even considered before. *I could take him back to my hostel. He doesn't know me. I don't know him. I'll never see him again, and that's okay.* Why not take what this man was so obviously offering? He didn't have to know that this wasn't something she ever did. "Please."

He ran one hand up her thigh, his heat seeming to brand itself through her jeans. "Tell me what you want."

A thousand answers flitted through her mind, but one dwarfed them all. Still, she hesitated. She'd just met him, and he was an ass—not exactly the prime candidate for someone to take to bed. But then he kissed down her neck, sucking on a spot that made the whole pub go blurry. God, how was she supposed to pass a man like him up? *It's just sex. It's not like I'm going to marry the man.* The Old Alexis wouldn't think to do this.

Which meant that was exactly what the New Alexis should do. She was supposed to be learning to take what she wanted. Right now, there was one need and one need alone dominating the forefront of her mind. She took a shuddering breath. "You. I want you."

"This wasn't supposed to happen." Before she could process his words, he kept going, his hand sliding a few inches higher, until he pressed against the vee of her legs. "But fuck, I'm not a saint. I never have been."

She didn't know what he was talking about, but it sounded like he was trying to convince himself to back off. *I just put myself out there for the first time* ever—*no way are we stopping.* There had to be something she could say to get his head back in the game. She tugged on his hair again, guiding him up until her lips brushed his with every word. "Take me now, Luke, or I'm going to walk out of this pub and find the first man who will." A bold-faced lie. If he rejected her, she'd walk back to her hostel with her tail between her legs. But in that moment, she almost believed herself. She wasn't the shy and polite and *obedient* Alexis. She was wild and free and could do whatever she damn well pleased.

Whomever she damn well pleased.

His eyes narrowed. "Like hell you will."

Oh, he didn't like that at all. Power, overwhelming as it was unfamiliar, swept over her. This man wasn't going to turn her down—not with that look on his face. From the sharp gleam in his green eyes, he appeared ready, willing, and able to follow through on their earlier conversation and haul her out of this bar. Oh *yes*.

She never thought she'd be into something like that. Sex had always been in the dark, beneath the covers, and completely as expected. She had a feeling sex with Luke wouldn't be *any* of those things.

She wanted that. She wanted him.

All she had to do was push him over the edge he was obviously teetering on. "Go ahead." Alexis dragged her nails over his jaw as she slid off his lap. "Call my bluff."

When he just sat on the stool, seeming to consider, a wave of apprehension rolled through her. Had she misjudged the whole situation? Embarrassment beat in time with her heart, scalding her skin. She took another step away, testing him, but he didn't move. Was he really going to let her walk out of here? The Old Alexis tried to surface, to do something to relieve the tension strung between them so tightly she could almost see it.

No. I'm not going to beg him to want me. I refuse to.

She lifted her chin and grabbed her pack off the floor. Pride might be the only thing she had left to herself, and she sure as hell wasn't going to sacrifice it *now*, to some man who meant less than nothing. She hadn't survived everything she had to break now.

With one last look at the still-unmoving Luke, she shook her head and started for the front door, refusing to glance over her shoulder. Over the years, she'd learned the hard way that looking back at what could have been was the best way to break her own heart. She'd duck around the corner and make her way back to the hostel and…take a cold shower or something. She most definitely wasn't hurt enough by his rejection to cry. That would be downright pathetic.

She barely made it out the door when she felt his presence at her back, unmistakable despite their minuscule time spent together. "Going somewhere?"

I wasn't wrong.

When was the last time her instincts had actually been correct? She couldn't remember and was grinning too hard to care. This was confirmation that the trip was the right answer. Two days, and she was already reclaiming a little piece of herself.

The night wasn't over yet. Forcing a disinterested expression onto her face, she turned around. God, he was magnificent. Tall and lean and glowering down at her like she'd gone and kicked his puppy. He wanted her, and he just as obviously didn't like that, and hell if that didn't make her whole night. She raised her eyebrows, unable to help poking at him. "I hear there's a place down the street where the local football team hangs out."

His brows slanted down, sending a delicious thrill through her. "You're testing my patience."

What is he waiting for? He was like a big, mean grizzly bear, and she had to be insane to want to go to bed with him. But she did. She wanted it more than she'd wanted anything in a very long time. *What will it take to push him over the edge?* Maybe she needed a really sharp stick. Obviously the thought of her jaunting off with another man—or multiple men—bothered him, so she'd just run with that. She shrugged. "You bought me a beer. I'm no longer your concern. Have a nice night."

Alexis got three steps before Luke swept her into his arms and tossed her over his shoulder. Her heavy backpack flopped down and smacked her in the back of the head. "What the hell?"

"You think I'm going to let some crazy soccer player strip you out of those jeans and taste you when you're wet for *me*? Not fucking likely, darlin'."

Yes. She grinned against his back, though she put as much snarl into her voice as she could. "Then stop running your mouth and actually do something about it."

Whatever intentions Luke had upon meeting Alexis had burned up in the attraction that flamed up between them. She thought she could just walk away and let some other man between those sweet thighs when they were shaking for *him*? The very idea made his blood pressure rise dangerously. She wanted him. She'd been all but begging for it when she was in his lap.

The time for hesitation was long gone. He turned his head to the side and sank his teeth into her ass, just hard enough to make her squirm. "Are you listening, darlin'?"

"Yes, goddamn it. Put me down and let me walk."

So she could walk away from him again? He tightened his grip, feeling like a man possessed. Reason reared its ugly head to point out he was carting around a woman he barely knew in a foreign city. *Damn it.* As much as he wanted to haul her back to his room and follow through on the promise of their kiss, the local authorities might label that kidnapping. She might have given him what he considered a green light—several, in fact—but it paid to be extremely clear in this scenario. With a growl, he set her on her feet. Alexis looked flushed and she was breathing heavily, but he needed more than that to move forward. He needed her words. "What do you want?"

"Why do you keep asking me that?" She pushed at his chest, her hair falling into her eyes. "Stop gloating and take me to bed."

Couldn't get much clearer than that. "It's not going to be nice, and it's not going to be sweet. If you want romance, you've got the wrong fucking man."

"No, really?" She glared at him, but her desire was written all over her face. "You're wasting both our time right now."

There wasn't much more he could do—except walk away. And that was the one thing he sure as hell wasn't going to do. He nodded once. "Come on." Luke took her hand and dragged her down the street, each step spiking the need and jealousy tangling in his system. These goddamn Irish guys would love to get their hands on a woman like this. Hell, the tourists in town would, too. And she was just going to waltz off and give away what should be his? A little voice whispered that he had no goddamn business thinking like that, but he told it to shut the fuck up.

He needed Alexis naked and in his bed, and he needed it now.

She stayed silent as they crossed the river, though her breath puffed out in the chilly night in her effort to keep up with him. His knee groaned in agony with each step, still not recovered from the combination of earlier hike and assault. Luke took a deep breath and forced himself to slow his pace. "Do you know what I'm going to do to you when I get you upstairs?"

"Tell me." No hesitation, no waffling, no threatening to go elsewhere.

It should have calmed him down a little. Instead, it only served to push him closer to the edge that was his hold on control. "After I get you out of those clothes, I'm going to sit you in my lap facing the mirror so you can see *exactly* who is driving you out of your mind. Those magnificent breasts of yours are practically begging for my attention, so I'll start there." The words felt forced out of him. He wanted to mark her, brand her, until she was as consumed with him as he was with her. "Then I'm going to spread those sweet thighs of yours and stroke you until you're begging for release."

"What if I don't beg?"

"Trust me, darlin', when I'm done with you, you're going to be on your knees and begging for my cock to fill your tight little pussy." A sound suspiciously close to a whimper came out of her, but when he looked back, she had that unflappable expression on her face that he was already starting to resent. Luke stopped walking and pulled her into his arms. "Don't believe me?"

She licked her lips and pressed against the front of his body. Christ, how was he supposed to make it back to the hotel with her body fitting so perfectly against his? Alexis slid her hand up his chest. "All I'm hearing is a lot of talk. Put your money where your mouth is."

Even as a small part of him admired her refusing to be railroaded, he wanted to curse her for not feeling as frantic as him. Luke grabbed her ass, using his hold to lift her until she pressed against his hard length. "Careful there, darlin', or I'm going to put my mouth on you right here." Her breath caught, and he allowed himself to grind on her one last time before he set her back on her feet. "We're almost there."

He focused on getting up to his room before he gave in to her challenge and put his money exactly where his mouth was. Who knew that all it took to drive him out of his damn mind was to have a woman who refused to pull her punches? She hadn't held back since she met him, and he sure as hell wasn't going to hold back now.

The elevator ride passed in a blur, and he towed her down the hall to his room. The door barely shut behind him when he pinned her against it. "You're mine now."

Even as she wrapped her legs around his waist, she

shook her head. "For tonight."

He wanted to rail against the limitation, but Luke was more concerned with getting her out of her clothes. With one punishing kiss, he moved to the bed and dropped her on it. Before she had a chance to right herself, he yanked off her boots and tossed them behind him. "Unbutton your pants."

"Bossy, bossy." But her voice was breathy, and her hands shook as she followed his order. He helped her get them over her hips and then peeled them off her legs, leaving her in only her white knit top and a thong with a shamrock that read *Lucky You.*

"Lucky me, indeed."

"Don't let it go to your head." She sat up, and he stripped off her shirt and bra. The panties could stay…for now. Alexis propped herself on her elbows and raised one slim leg to poke him in the chest with her foot when he started to crawl onto the bed. "Your turn."

All he could see was her smooth skin and dark pink nipples. When she poked him again, he finally focused on her face. "What?"

"Your clothes. Get rid of them."

For the first time since he'd kissed her, Luke paused. He hadn't been with anyone in a long time. Hell, he could pinpoint the exact time because the woman had taken one look at his mangled knee and taken off. And that was *after* she cringed at the sight of his scars elsewhere. He couldn't stand the thought of Alexis flinching from him. "Not yet."

First, he was going to drive her so far out of her mind with pleasure that she wouldn't have the ability to remember her own name, let alone worry about his damaged body.

Chapter Four

Alexis didn't get a chance to argue, because Luke grabbed her ankle and towed her closer. "Do you remember what I told you?"

How could she forget? It felt like every word he'd said on their way from Sin É to his hotel was branded on her skin. It had been everything she could do to keep her wits about her and her replies snarky instead of breathless. If he'd made a move, she wasn't sure she would have had the strength to tell him to wait until they got back to his room—and even now she wasn't sure if she'd have cared if he'd taken her right there in the street. *Dorothy, we are not in Kansas anymore.*

Luke was obviously still waiting for an answer, so she nodded. "I remember."

"Tell me."

He was going to make her say it? It was one thing to listen to it from a man who made her blood heat—it was entirely another to speak it herself. She shifted, trying to pull her ankle out of his grip. "You're still wearing too many clothes."

"Changing the subject won't distract me, darlin'." He gave another tug, bringing her to the end of the bed. "What am I going to do to you?"

She swallowed hard, acutely aware that she was nearly naked and he was still fully clothed and watching her as if he would drink her down. She'd never talked dirty before, but this entire trip was about new experiences and taking life by the horns. She could do this. All she had to do was open her mouth and speak. "You said…"

He waited, his thumb tracing maddening circles on her ankle. God, he really wasn't going to give an inch. Alexis cleared her throat. "You said you would strip me down, sit me on your lap, and drive me crazy…" Her gaze landed on the dresser across from the bed. Sure enough, it had a giant mirror on top of it. *Oh wow.* "Where I could see exactly who was touching me." She could already picture how it would look, his big hands on her body, spreading her and stoking her desire and driving her out of her mind. Hell, he had her halfway there and he had barely touched her yet.

Maybe there was something to be said for this dirty talking stuff.

Luke's eyes seemed to darken. "And afterward I'm going to press you against that window and fuck you from behind where anyone who looks up can see you."

She whipped around so fast, she almost fell off the bed. As distracted as she was, she hadn't noticed the floor-to-ceiling windows taking up the wall opposite the door. Heat spread through her body at the thought of him pressing her against that window. She'd never thought of herself as an exhibitionist, but she was leaving Cork tomorrow, so it wasn't as if she'd run into someone who'd see the peep show.

Or the man who planned to put her on display.

The thought sent a pang through her, which she promptly ignored. Luke was hot as hell, but he and she could barely sit next to each other for two minutes without making painfully snarky comments. This wasn't meant to last more than a night. This wasn't even about him, not really. This was about her taking back control of her life. Though if she only had tonight, she sure as hell intended to make it count. "Yes."

"Yes?"

"Yes. I want that."

"Darlin', I wasn't asking your permission." He went to his knees in front of her and used his hands to spread her legs wider. "You're going to love every single thing I do to you tonight."

"And if I don't?" Not that she doubted him, but she didn't exactly have a stellar track record when it came to being intimate. Her ex-fiancé, Eric, had called her boring and bemoaned the loss of the woman he'd had before her. Just another way she'd been a disappointment.

She couldn't stand the thought of seeing that same look in Luke's eyes, even if she was pretty sure she didn't actually *like* him. Once again, the Old Alexis tried to wrestle back into control. *What am I doing here with this man I barely know? This could be a horrible mistake. He's going to be disappointed in me, just like everyone else I come into contact with.*

"Open your eyes, darlin'."

Alexis hadn't realized she'd closed them to begin with. She hesitated to obey, fearing what she might see on his face, but there was no denying the command in his voice. Feeling a whole lot like she was about to face the firing squad, she opened her eyes.

He frowned. "Whatever is going through your head right now, let it go."

Let it go? If she knew how to do that, she never would have needed this trip to begin with. "Easier said than done."

This was it. This was where he'd shake his head and stand up, or maybe go pleasure himself in the shower because apparently that was preferable to her in his bed. She started to pull away, to do something to protect herself from the pending rejection. Though really, there was nothing she could do to combat the sting. She'd learned that through far too many experiences.

Luke's brows dropped, the forbidding expression strangely comforting. "Guess that just means I need to step up my game." His fingers dug into her thighs, and she couldn't stifle a gasp of surprise.

Before she could reconcile reality with what was happening in her head, he leaned down and pressed an open-mouthed kiss to her whisper-thin panties. She sat bolt upright as if he'd hit her with a cattle prod. While she was trying to relearn how to breathe, Luke nuzzled her panties to the side and dragged his tongue over her center.

Oh my God, this is really happening. He hadn't walked away, and he hadn't rejected her. He was here between her thighs, his mouth on the most private part of her as if he'd never tasted anything as decadent.

A whimper slipped free as he did it again. He paused and met her gaze, the fire in his green eyes searing her to the core. "You taste like peaches here, too."

"I—"

"Darlin', as flattered as I am that you're trying to talk right now, the only thing I want to hear is you screaming my name." He leaned back long enough to pull her panties off, and then he was back, spreading her legs up and out, baring her completely. "Fucking beautiful."

As he went to work exploring her with his mouth, she didn't have the breath to point out…anything. Instead she let herself fall back on the bed and be consumed with how good his mouth felt on her. But one thought resonated even through the delirious pleasure he was drawing from her body.

No one has ever called me beautiful before.

Luke couldn't get enough of her taste—or the noises coming out of her mouth with each lick. She writhed and moaned as if she'd never had a man take his time and savor her like this. The thought that maybe no man had before him drove the possessive feeling he had no right to higher. As selfish as it was, he wanted to be the one she never forgot, the one she compared every sexual encounter to for the rest of her privileged life. Even considering her with other men made him growl against her skin. The jealousy taking the steering wheel was as out of place as the possessiveness, but he couldn't have stopped if he wanted to. And he sure as fuck didn't want to.

"Who's making you feel like this?" When she just moaned louder, he set his teeth against her clit. "Say it."

"You are." She laced her fingers through his hair, her

hips jerking against his mouth until he had to pin her to the bed. The move only drove her wilder, her moans turning into cries that evolved into his name. "Luke, oh my God, oh, oh, oh, *Luke*."

"That's right, darlin'. Me." He gentled his kisses until her shaking stilled, and then raised his head. Whatever dark thoughts had plagued her earlier were gone now. Because of *him*. Alexis watched him through eyes gone dark with passion, and though she looked sated, her gaze dropped to his mouth. *Not quite sated yet.* With a grin, he crawled onto the bed next to her. "You're not done."

It took her two tries to smile, but she somehow managed. "Good thing. I was sure you were a one-trick pony."

He laughed. God help him, but he liked that the princess had claws. Even if half the time, she was sinking them into him. "Lord, woman, you always have a comeback ready, don't you?"

A frown flickered over her face. "Not always."

There it was again—whatever imagined burden she carried, trying to force its way back to the forefront of her mind. He was more than intimate with exactly how that shit worked. It struck him that he didn't really know much about her, other than the fact that her sister and friends didn't think she could handle herself alone in Europe. What *hadn't* they told him before they sent him off on this protection mission?

It didn't matter. Her worries could wait for another day. Tonight, Alexis was his.

He hooked the back of her neck and kissed her. Her hands immediately went to his hair again, which would have amused him if he weren't half a second from ripping off his pants and sinking into her. Once again, reality spoke up.

Luke broke away with a curse. "Condoms."

"What?"

"I don't have goddamn condoms." The one thing he hadn't prepared for, because this was supposed to be a babysitting mission, and one did not fuck around on a babysitting mission.

Unless, apparently, one did.

Alexis's eyes cleared. "Oh, I do."

He went still, refusing to move when she pushed against his shoulder. "What?"

"Condoms. I have them in my pack."

"Why in God's name would you have condoms in your pack?" He didn't care that it saved them a trip to the market down the street. All that mattered was that she'd planned on having sex with someone. The thought of her with someone else made him crazy, and he had the totally insane need to mark her as his. It wasn't some other man here, chasing the shadows away. It was *him*.

She watched him with an unreadable expression on her face. "I like to be prepared."

"Prepared to let some idiot soccer player between your thighs." As he spoke, he pinned her wrists above her head.

"Has anyone ever told you that you're unnaturally obsessed with soccer players?" She rolled her eyes, her levity calming him a little. "You sure you're not harboring some guy-on-guy tendencies?"

Luke didn't get it. He'd never once, in all his thirty-three years, reacted like this. He was the jokester, the one who ran his mouth, the footloose and fancy-free friend who was good for a bang and then moved on before anyone could get attached. Or at least, he had been, before his injury.

He didn't get jealous, let alone *this*, whatever the fuck this emotion could be called. "Alexis—"

Her eyes went hard, and he could practically hear her claws unsheathing. "Don't you dare! Whatever the hell you're about to say, just shut up. I'm here, naked, with *you*. Tonight I'm yours, and you're wasting it worrying about what-if scenarios that are, frankly, none of your business."

He didn't miss the part where she limited this to tonight. "Look—"

"No, *you* look. I already came against your mouth. Are you really going to talk this to death?"

She was right. Tonight was for leaving all their baggage behind. Hell, this couldn't go further than sex, because he could barely stand to be in the same room with her under the best of circumstances. That feeling wasn't going to get better when he was chasing her ass all over Europe. Luke kissed her again, pushing all his annoyance and issues from his head. She was right. They were his problems—not hers.

There was only the here and now. When he finally broke away, they were both breathing hard. "You better not plan on sleeping tonight."

"I wouldn't dream of it."

Chapter Five

Alexis yanked the box of condoms from her pack and thanked God she'd been optimistic enough to bring them in the first place. A truly impressive dry spell and crippling self-doubt didn't exactly lend themselves to hot one-night stands… Or so she'd thought before she met Luke. A lot of things she'd previously thought were hard truths didn't seem to hold up to the harsh light of his presence.

He pulled her back to the bed and into his lap. As promised, they faced the mirror, where she could see nearly her entire body and meet his eyes. The sheer intimacy of the position was totally and completely unexpected, and she wasn't sure she liked it. "Why don't we skip straight to the window?"

"Nice try." He hooked her thighs and spread them to the outside of his legs, using his knees to open her even wider. After plucking the condoms from her hand and dropping them on the bed, he reached around her to cup her breasts.

"Perfect, just like the rest of you."

The insane urge to argue with him rose. *I'm not perfect. I'm so flawed and broken, it isn't even funny.* Some days she was half surprised that her issues weren't there on her body, marked out for all to see. "Actually—"

"Woman, enough." He pinched her nipples, sending a zing of sheer lust through her that stole her breath. "I don't need your pretty-girl insecurities clouding up the moment. I say you're perfect, and that means you're fucking perfect. The only thing I should hear from you in response is 'thank you.' Understand?"

She licked her lips. Part of her still wanted to argue with him, but it was the Old Alexis creeping in. He was right—arguing with him over something like this was stupid. "Yes."

"Now, where were we?" He squeezed her breasts one last time before smoothing his hands down her sides and over her thighs. As she watched, one hand dipped to drag a finger over her glistening center. She could actually *see* how wet she was from here, and Alexis couldn't help shifting and trying to close her thighs. Luke, of course, was having none of it. "I like seeing you, darlin'." He spread her folds and worked a finger into her. "Christ, you're tight. Haven't let another man inside in a long time, have you?"

She tried to lift her hips as a second finger joined his first, but he easily held her in place. Admitting that it had been well over a year and a half since she was with anyone would give him too much ammunition to use against her. Even as the thought crossed her mind, she gave herself a mental shake. What did it matter if Luke knew he was the only one in recent memory? It wasn't as if she'd stick around long enough for the inevitable barbs. "Not since my ex-fiancé. Eighteen months."

He cursed again and then pressed a kiss to her neck as he worked her with his fingers. "I'm going to make it good for you, darlin'. So fucking good that no one else can compare."

Empty threats. She hoped.

Whatever his faults, Luke saw her as a woman—and a woman he wanted so badly he couldn't seem to get enough of touching her. *A beautiful, sexy woman.* For tonight, she could set her issues aside and maybe even see herself that way, too.

Not to mention, he made her feel too good to stop. *Stop thinking so much and just* feel. She let her head fall back to rest on his shoulder, but kept her eyes open so she could see exactly what his hands were doing. When in doubt, she fell back to the attitude that had gotten him to haul her back here in the first place. "There you go again, making threats you have no way of following through on."

His laughter rumbled against her back. "I'll pick up that gauntlet you just threw at my feet." Before she could respond, he twisted his wrist, hitting that spot just inside her, and used his other hand to stroke over her clit. "But first, you're coming for me. Again."

She tried to move, to arch, to do something, but his arms around her held her pinned against his chest. All she could do was take the pleasure he gave her and watch his fingers slide in and out of her as his circled her clit. "Oh God."

"That's right, darlin'. Almost there, aren't you?"

"*Yes.*" She twisted blindly, and he obligingly gave her his mouth. Or more accurately, he took her mouth much the same way he was taking her pleasure. Luke's tongue thrust between her lips in the same rhythm as his fingers into her body. She was poised on the precipice, the desire rising in her body almost too much to bear. "Please. Oh God, *please*, Luke."

"I've got you." He did something with his fingers that sent her hurtling under, screaming his name. All Alexis could do was cling to him as her orgasm took over, shivers ripping through her body. He stopped stroking her, but kept his hand between her legs, cupping her in a move that screamed possessive male. When she finally managed to pry her eyes open, his green eyes were focused on her face, as if drinking in every little reaction.

She slouched against him, boneless with pleasure, though her body already pulsed with a building need. As good as that had been, she needed him filling her, needed to have his bare skin against hers. "Luke—"

"Hush." He kissed her again. "Enjoy the afterglow. We're not even close to done yet."

Now was the time to take off his clothes, when Alexis was languid with pleasure. Luke took a deep breath, trying to fight down the stupid insecurity. If he kept his clothes on, that would bring even more attention to the bullshit inside his head than if he just stripped and got it over with—but that meant letting her get a look at his scars. Fuck, he'd never been this kind of a coward before that IED, and he wasn't about to start now.

He pulled off his shirt and wasn't able to contain a groan when her smooth back pressed against his bare chest. It had been so goddamn long since he'd touched another person like this, skin on skin, that it was almost painful. He wrapped his arms around her and tried to adjust to it. But she was already shifting, rocking her ass against his cock. To hell with this idiocy. He scooted her forward enough to unbutton his jeans and then held onto her as he jerked them down and kicked them off. It wasn't smooth and it wasn't pretty, but the end result made both of them moan.

As he rolled a condom on, he couldn't keep his eyes off her in the mirror. He hadn't been lying when he called her body perfection. She was so beautiful it actually hurt to look at her, a sharp stabbing pain somewhere in the vicinity of his chest that made him want to both look away and never take his eyes off her. The fact that she didn't seem to agree was baffling, though not unexpected when he really thought about it. Very few women looked in the mirror and saw reality, and it was a damn shame.

"No more waiting." Alexis lifted herself and reached down to position him at her entrance. "Now, Luke." She barely glanced down at his knee and its mass of scar tissue.

"As you wish, darlin'." He grabbed her hips and brought her down as he thrust up, sheathing himself to the hilt. "*Christ.*" Even his stretching her earlier hadn't done a whole lot. She was so tight he had to press his forehead to the back of her neck to keep himself from blowing right then and there.

"You feel so good." She tried to move, but he kept their hips sealed. "God, Luke, I need to move. Please."

He lifted her and brought her back down slowly, watching as his cock disappeared inside her. When he raised his gaze, he found her eyes pinned to the same spot, and she bit her lip with each upward thrust. "You like that. Seeing me fuck you. Watching my cock slide into your wet little pussy."

"*Yes*."

"You want me to pin you against that window, where anyone can see those perfect pink nipples pressed against the glass. You *want* people to see."

A shudder passed through her body. "I—"

"Tell me the truth, darlin'."

She looked up and met his gaze in the mirror, her hazel eyes a little dazed. "I want you to take me against the window."

"And you're going to come knowing everyone in the street below can see you."

Her breath hissed out. "Yes."

Fuck, he was about to come just talking about it. Or maybe it was the squeeze of her around him, fluttering with each word he spoke. He lifted her off his cock and stood, walking them to the space where the curtains parted. They hadn't bothered to turn on any lights when they came through the door, relying on the single lamp next to the bed, so he wasn't worried that anyone would actually see more than the outline of Alexis against the window. As hot as it seemed to get her knowing that anyone could see them, he wasn't about to put her on display for the whole of Cork.

He guided her hands to the glass on either side of her head. "Don't move these."

She gave a husky laugh. "There you go again, thinking you're the boss."

"Darlin', tonight I am." He refused to think of after tonight, when he had to deal with the consequences of what he was in the process of doing. Luke kicked her feet farther apart and reached between her legs. "You're so damn wet.

You love this."

"Maybe."

"No maybe about it. Your body doesn't lie." He couldn't resist sliding a finger into her before he bent his knees and replaced it with his cock. The position wasn't a comfortable one for his knee, but he could give a flying fuck when she made a sweet little cry. He twined her long hair around one fist and bent her backward, the move pressing her breasts against the glass and allowing him to push deeper. He shoved into her, the crazed feeling returning, as if he couldn't get deep enough, couldn't get enough of her, couldn't do anything but chase the pressure building in the small of his back. "This is what you want, isn't it?"

"Yes. Oh God, don't stop."

"I won't." He shoved into her again and used his free hand to reach around and stroke her clit. "Not until you're coming around my cock."

She arched her back, taking him deeper. "Good."

She was almost there. The sounds coming out of her mouth were indication of that, the same way she went wild around him. Luke gritted his teeth and kept up his pace, determined to see her come one more time before he gave in to his own oblivion. "Now, darlin'. I know you're close. Come for me now."

"*Luke*." She shuddered, her pussy milking his cock, stealing away his control. He grabbed her hips and pounded into her, needing his release as much as he'd needed hers. His orgasm tore through him, making his knee buckle. Luke caught them both at the last second, but he had to brace himself on the glass and with an arm around her waist to keep them off the floor. "Fuck."

"I can't even..."

Yeah, him either. He hadn't expected this. Even when he was tossing her ass over his shoulder, he hadn't really considered that the sex would be mind-blowing.

When she started to straighten, he tightened his grip, not ready to break their contact yet. At some point he was going to have to face that he'd made a mess of things, but he wasn't ready to. Not yet. "Where do you think you're going?"

"A shower?"

"Not fucking likely. I'm not done with you yet." He picked her up and set her on the couch next to the windows. After tossing the condom in the garbage, he knelt in front of her and spread her legs.

Her eyes went wide. "Again?"

"Woman, I'm haven't had even close to enough of you." He leaned down and sucked her clit into his mouth. "I hope you don't have any plans until tomorrow afternoon, because you're going to miss them."

Chapter Six

Alexis woke up as the sun hit the curtains across the room. She stretched, loving how sore and used her body felt. True to his word, Luke made sure she didn't get much sleep at all last night. He lay sprawled next to her, his head buried in his pillow. She propped herself up on her elbows and finally allowed herself to look her fill. Last night, he'd done a damn good job of making sure she was so distracted, she couldn't get a good view of his body. When they'd finally collapsed in bed together, he tucked them both in and flipped off the lamp inside of ten seconds. It was unreal.

As she shifted the sheet to the side, she realized why. An angry scar wound its way down his side to his leg before exploding over his knee. The flesh looked strange, as if it'd been grafted in. *That's exactly what it is*, she realized. Something had torn into him with such violence that she couldn't imagine there was much left of this leg when it was through with him. Considering what she knew of the war overseas, it had to be an IED.

When he'd given her the curt answer about his knee last night, she'd pegged him for military. Apparently she was right.

Something inside her softened to think of the pain and agony he must have gone through—was still going through, if his limp was any indication. It didn't excuse his shitty attitude—plenty of men walked away with worse injuries and managed to still see the cup as half full—but it gave her an unwelcome insight to everything Luke. She didn't like it. This was so much easier to chalk up to a stranger in a strange land who blew her mind and, as a result, gave her back a little sliver of what she'd been missing for so long.

A step in the right direction.

She glanced at the clock next to the bed and mentally cursed. She'd have to hurry or she was going to miss her flight. Plus, she wanted to call and check in with Avery. Maybe apologize for skipping town before the baby shower.

Even thinking about it had her throat closing. Her sister hadn't done anything the "right" way—planning to use her best friend as a sperm donor and go it alone, despite the plan nearly giving *Yé-yé* a coronary—but she'd still managed to find happiness with her now-fiancé. And they were expecting a baby, the one thing Alexis had wanted more than anything in the world.

The one thing that was forever beyond her reach.

She'd survived the same cancer that killed her mother, but the cost had been so goddamn high. Her ability to have children, her potential marriage with Eric, the acceptance of her traditional Chinese grandparents. All of it taken away with the surgery that ended up saving her life.

She supposed she should feel lucky to be alive, but on the dark days, when her grandfather was telling her what a failure of a woman she was, she had a hell of a time appreciating that fact. All she could see was the stark reality of what she'd lost.

Maybe if Mom were still alive, she would see things differently. Her mother had died when she was sixteen, but she'd been bright and full of life right up to the very end, even when the end itself was unavoidable. Alexis hadn't managed that. The cancer was gone, but she couldn't shake the feeling that she'd lost something irreplaceable along the way.

She sat up. God, she shouldn't be dwelling on any of these things. She was in Ireland—a land of magic and possibilities, where being in the right place at the right time was enough to shove a person into a whole different world. And hadn't she stumbled onto both with this rough-and-tumble man who made her forget her own name? The past shouldn't be able to shoulder its way into the now and leech any happiness she had as a result of him...but it did.

Time to go.

She dressed as quietly as possible and paused by the dresser mirror that he'd pleasured her in front of last night. Her body heated from the memory, and she managed to dredge up a smile. Her time in Cork had been positive, even if her emotional baggage hadn't magically disappeared as a result. She'd found someone who actually saw her as a woman—a sexy woman. That was a gift she'd never forget.

This is only the first step. I'm moving in the right direction, and that's all that matters. Luke was part of that, and I'll always cherish this memory.

She scrawled a quick note onto the hotel stationery before she walked out the door.

A few blocks down from the hotel, she found a pay phone that would serve her purpose. After jumping through the necessary hoops for an international call, she held her breath while it rang. Maybe Avery wouldn't pick up. That would be easier. She'd drop a "Hey, I'm still alive" voicemail and go catch a plane.

Of course, the universe wasn't feeling so accommodating.

"Hello?"

She closed her eyes, a wave of homesickness rolling over her that was so intense it almost brought her to her knees. Through all her hills and valleys and life repeatedly kicking her in the teeth, her sister had been one of the constants. She'd never left Alexis's side, never hesitated in her belief that her older sister would get through the treatments and come out victorious. Alexis swallowed hard. "Hey."

"*Alexis?* Oh my God, where are you? We've been so worried! You disappeared and all you left was a text saying not to worry about you. What the hell is with that?" There was a smacking noise. "Yes, Drew, it's Alexis. No, I don't know where she is. If you'll just shut up for half a second, I'll get some answers." Avery cleared her throat. "Where are you?"

Now was not the time to falter. Even if her issues had popped up to punch her in the face this morning, her overall experience in Cork had been enough to prove she was right to take this trip in the first place. "Europe. I have some things I need to do, but I'll be home…when I'm home. Before the baby." That, at least, she could promise. She wouldn't let her personal crap get in the way of being there when her niece or nephew came into the world.

"Wow, that's some serious detail you're giving me. How about you try again?"

It wouldn't hurt to give her a little information. It wasn't like there was a whole lot Avery could do with it, being pregnant and all. No way would Drew let her catch a flight here—and he wouldn't leave her, either. Not to mention, it was selfish to leave them completely hanging. She took a deep breath. "Remember that cliff that's been my screen saver for the last six months?"

"The one in Norway that scares you shitless even looking at it?"

"That's the one." Another breath. "I'm going to hike up there and see it."

"*Why?* You're terrified of skyscrapers, and that's a whole lot higher. What are you trying to prove, Alexis?"

There it was, the thing her sister didn't understand. Avery had been scared enough of losing her ability to have biological children that she took matters into her own hands and made life mold to her expectations. There was no obstacle she couldn't look at and figure out a way to overcome.

Alexis had never had that kind of courage. No, that wasn't true. She'd been downright fearless growing up. But then Mom died and everything changed. Her dad did the best he could, but he wasn't Mom. And then *Yé-yé* and *Nâi-nai* moved in and took over.

Some days she felt like she'd just been going through the motions since then. She needed this, needed a reset button, to get her life figured out so she didn't go to her deathbed wishing she'd made different choices. The first step had been Ireland with its magic and population that was so in love with life, it was hard for some of it not to rub off on her. Just like Mom had described.

Next, it was time to face her fears. If there was nothing left to be afraid of, maybe she could start to reclaim her life the way their mother would have wanted her to. She'd spent so long dancing to other people's tunes, it was a foreign concept.

Alexis bit her lip. It wasn't about proving something. It was about reclaiming herself. She couldn't set that aside, even for her sister. "I love you, Avery. Give Drew a kiss for me. I'll call in a few days or a week or something." She hung up before her sister could say anything else. There was nothing to say. The decision had already been made. She was here, and she was going to see this through.

Luke woke up to the sound of his satellite phone ringing. He rolled over, reaching for Alexis and coming up empty. Only then did he open his eyes. Empty bed, empty room, open door to a dark bathroom. She was gone. And he had no idea where she was staying, so it wasn't like he could camp out in front of her hotel and wait for the princess to show herself. He'd well and truly fucked up. "Shit." He rolled back over and grabbed the phone. "Yeah?"

"Where the hell are you?"

Flannery. He closed his eyes and collapsed back onto the bed. "You know where I am. You're the one who booked my ticket." And now he had to admit that he'd had a line on Alexis and let her get away because he was too tired from fucking her all night to wake up when she slipped out.

On second thought, maybe he'd leave out that last part.

"And now you're making jokes."

Because he didn't have it in him to do much else. Every part of his body hurt from the hike yesterday and what he'd done to Alexis last night. He wanted to roll over and go back to sleep for a few hours, but that wasn't in the itinerary—not when she'd ghosted on him. "I lost her."

"No shit. I knew that before you did, apparently."

He opened his eyes. Flannery knew where she was? What the hell had changed between yesterday when they'd only known she booked a flight for Cork and now? "How?"

"She called her sister. They only talked for a few minutes, but it was enough for her to let us know where she's headed."

That got him moving. Luke stood, and flinched when his knee voiced a protest. Stupid goddamn injury. He wouldn't let it slow him down. He couldn't. "Tell me."

"Look, I wouldn't have asked you to do this if I thought you couldn't handle it. But…what the hell happened?"

What happened was that he'd been assaulted, and then turned around and lost his head over this woman. It crossed his mind that she was onto why he was here and had played him, but he dismissed the thought. If she knew he'd been sent to keep her safe, she would have given him a piece of her mind and told him where to shove it. That said, he wasn't about to tell Flannery how badly he'd botched protection duty. "She just got away from me. Where is she headed?"

Flannery hesitated so long, he was half sure the man would call him off the whole mission. "Norway."

The problem with Europe was that it had far too many places within easy reach. He had a list of destinations where Avery thought her sister might go, but nothing more than his best guess at the order. Norway hadn't even been on the fucking list. "What the hell is she after in Norway?"

"Ever hear of Pulpit Rock? It's called Preikestolen locally."

No, but he was about to get educated. "Why wasn't this on the list of possible places she'd go?"

"Because it's a goddamn mountain, and her sister is afraid of heights."

More self-discovery shit? Of course. "Where do I need to fly in?"

"Stavanger."

Good enough. He'd read up on his way. "I'll be on the next flight out."

"Thanks, man." Again, a hesitation. "Thank you for doing this. We're all really worried about her."

Which only drove home that there was something Flannery wasn't telling him. She might be a princess, but he still had a hard time wrapping his head around the fact that she knew she had people worried sick about her, and she'd just dropped everything and taken off. Normal people planned a trip like this, gave their family an itinerary with the expected day they'd be back, and *then* flew to Europe.

He hesitated, torn between wanting to know what the hell was going on and not wanting to waste any more time on this phone call. "You didn't tell me a whole lot about her when you called for help." And he'd owed Flannery enough that he hadn't bothered to ask. Now Luke was wondering if that had been a mistake.

"She's important to us, and we're worried about her. I wasn't aware you needed a goddamn profile."

He didn't, not if his only goal was to keep her safe. He shoved down his irritation. Mostly. "Don't worry about it. I'll keep her out of trouble." He hung up.

Yeah, he'd keep her out of trouble, but she was going to get an earful when he found her. Who the hell did she think she was, bouncing out on him like he was some kind of dirty one-night stand?

The fact that she'd been up-front about calling them exactly that didn't change a damn thing.

Luke stopped next to the dresser, his gaze falling to the piece of paper there. There was no explanation, no way to get a hold of her, just a hastily written, *You gave me back a piece of what I was looking for. Thank you.* Yet another indication that he was swimming in deep waters, and no one had thought to warn him that there were sharks about. *What the hell is she running from?* He frowned at the note. *Or running toward?* He wanted to rip it up and flush it down the toilet, but he stuffed it in his pocket instead.

He had a plane to Norway to catch.

Chapter Seven

Two motherfucking miles. Luke cursed again as his knee cried out. Two miles *up*. Because apparently Alexis the Princess simply *had* to climb to the top of a goddamn cliff and stare off it. Maybe she was calling in the birds from the area to do her cleaning à la her Disney counterparts, or she just wanted to feel closer to nature, but Christ, she could do either of those things on flat ground that didn't require him to bust his ass up a path…

He stumbled to a stop, looked up…and kept looking. "You have got to be fucking with me." The path turned into a goddamn mountain, so steep he'd have to use both his feet and his hands to climb, and it was riddled with boulders. He'd be lucky if he made it to the top without spraining an ankle.

This all could have been bypassed if he'd caught an earlier flight. But the early one—the same one he suspected Alexis was on out of Cork—had already left by the time he made it to the airport. So he was stuck with the evening flight. By the time he made it to Stavanger, it was well past dinnertime, and he had no idea where she would have picked to spend the night. The helpful stewardess had told him that the hike to Pulpit Rock—or Preikestolen as most people called it—was an all-day event. So at least he'd been spared from chasing after her in the dark.

Which was why he was here, at the ass-crack of dawn, ready to risk permanent injury to get to the top of this shit. If Alexis had kept on the phone long enough to tell her sister where she was staying, this would have been unnecessary, but noooooo.

He leaned down to rub his knee, knowing damn well that his anger was misplaced. It didn't make it miraculously disappear to know the source was a combination of the physical aggravation from his knee and his bruised pride from the fact that she'd slipped out of bed without him so much as stirring.

He'd dropped the ball.

Luke braced himself for the pain that was about to become his world and started up. Faced with this challenge, he couldn't help thinking that this would have been an easy hike before that IED blew off half his right leg. He would have spent it joking and laughing. Now… Now, it was a struggle to take the next step.

And hell if the reminder of all the ways his life was different didn't piss him off. He wasn't whole anymore. If he had been, the Air Force would have kept him on as a pararescuer. But he couldn't meet the physical requirements—he didn't even come close the one time he'd tried. To do his job, he had to be at the top of his game, and that's something he never would be again.

By the time he hit the halfway point, he was breathing hard, and his leg shook with the effort. Pathetic. If he were smart, he'd stop and rest his knee for a little bit. He kept going, because the sad truth was that if he stopped now, he was going to have a hard time getting started again. Better to just muscle through it and hope that the trip down would be less difficult.

He glanced up, thankful that the dark clouds overhead had kept all but the most determined tourists off the trail. He didn't want an audience for this. As it was, he got pitying looks as a group of chatting girls bypassed him. One fact solidified in his mind as his knee screamed from the effort of hauling himself upward.

This was Alexis's fault.

Not his weakness, but having to put it on display. He bet she'd just bounded up this hill, marveling at how wonderful the world was. Spoiled-rotten princess.

That's not fair and you know it.

Yeah, he did. He didn't feel a whole lot like being fair right now. When he got to the top of this beast, he wasn't sure if he was going to kiss the hell out of her or yell until he was blue in the face.

The path opened in front of him, leveling out to the cliff itself, a wide, flat rock that overlooked the fjord from a truly impressive height. The shock of it had him stumbling to a stop. Even though the path upward was brutal, it was closed in enough that he hadn't realized how high up they were until now. It would be a brutal drop if someone went over the edge. And Europeans weren't worried about putting safety cables or fences in place to keep some idiot from taking a running leap into oblivion if they were so inclined. Maybe they saw it as a way of natural selection, but it didn't do a damn thing for his blood pressure.

But even with that staggering beauty in front of him, his attention zeroed in on Alexis and stayed there. She stood alone between two groups of people, and even from this distance he could see her face lifted and her eyes closed. Inexplicably, she wore a sundress with her hiking boots. His mind flashed back to the climb he'd just done, and he couldn't help imagining how much easier it would have been if he had a view up that dress to keep him motivated.

But seriously, who the hell wore a sundress to hike a cliff? Obviously someone with no connection to reality.

He started to take a step forward when her shoulders squared. She looked like she was about to march into a battle, like she was steeling herself for something terrible. Luke looked around, frowning when he didn't see anything particularly terrifying. What was she doing?

Flannery had said she was afraid of heights. Not that he'd believed it, knowing Alexis scaled this bitch. This mountain was wicked *steep.* Alexis picked up her pack and took a cautious step forward—toward the edge of the cliff. He could actually see her take a deep breath and then force herself another step forward.

She's terrified. Fear screamed from every line of her body, seeming to get more intense the closer she got to the edge. She staggered to a stop about six feet from the cliff, her shoulders so tense, it looked like she might break into a million pieces. But she didn't retreat. She didn't move forward any more, but she didn't back away, either.

Against all reason, a slow appreciation wound through him. He knew about facing fears—he'd spent most of his two years of training for the PJs doing just that. Yeah, he'd been afraid of drowning and failing his patient instead of something so mundane as heights, but that didn't make the courage she showed any less real.

But it couldn't be clearer that fear had her all locked up. She looked like a rabbit in the face of a wolf, frozen and hoping the danger would pass if she didn't move. *You can do it, princess. You have claws. Use them.* A minute passed, and then another. If someone didn't do something, she'd be here all night. Or worse, she'd talk herself away from the edge. He didn't climb all the way up here for her to back out. Luke cursed under his breath and started for her.

Alexis could barely breathe past the panic fluttering in her veins. So high. It had been scary climbing up here, because the urge to turn around and see exactly how far she'd ascended was nearly overwhelming. But the closed-in feeling of the path had helped steady her. Now there was nothing but wide-open spaces at the top.

Six feet from the edge, frozen in terror, the sheer drop to the water of the fjord nearly two thousand feet below… *Actually, it's 1,982 feet.* "Oh God." A few more feet and she'd be at the edge, within reach of that paralyzing drop. It was all too tempting to shake off her fear and back away. The only person she was trying to prove something to was herself—it wasn't like she was going to disappoint anyone if she didn't touch the edge of Pulpit Rock.

Anyone but herself.

If she couldn't do even this, then what the hell was she

doing in Europe to begin with? *This isn't any harder than what I've spent the last few years going through—than what Mom went through. If she could do that, I should be able to take these last few steps and touch the edge.* The only thing standing in her way was her fear.

But the fear was an overwhelmingly physical thing. It clawed down her throat and through her chest, making her skin feel too tight and her breath come too fast. *I have to be sedated for plane rides. What the hell was I thinking hiking up here?*

She was thinking she wanted to put Old Alexis in the dust. Climbing to the top of a cliff, let alone one that had a two-thousand-foot drop off the end of it, wasn't even in the realm of possibilities a few months ago. And she was here. She'd made it to the top. Now she just needed to take the last few steps and banish the mousy part of her that would rather go with the flow than rock the boat, once and for all.

Mom would have walked out there without hesitation.

Yeah, well, Mom wasn't afraid of heights. Mom wasn't afraid of *anything*.

"What the fuck do you think you're doing?"

She almost ignored the words, sure that the angry man on the other end couldn't be talking to her, but she *knew* that voice. Intimately. Alexis looked over her shoulder and, for one eternal second, she was sure she was experiencing a fear-based hallucination. Because there was no other way to explain the sight of Luke bearing down on her, storms in his green eyes. Except then he was in front of her and glowering in that way she was already coming to recognize.

She blinked, but he didn't disappear. "What are you doing here?"

"I have a better question. What are you trying to prove?"

She stared, not liking the way he gave voice to the very same question she'd just been thinking. "What?"

For a second, he hesitated, but then his brows dropped. "Christ, princess, I'm not even using big words—what are you trying to prove by crawling up here in that sad excuse for hiking gear? World's prettiest thrill-seeker, too afraid to even look over the edge of a cliff?"

Anger straightened her spine, and she took her first full breath since she reached the summit. *How dare he? He doesn't know a damn thing about me.* What happened in Cork didn't give him free rein to steamroll all over her. Speaking of Cork… "Says the man who's stalking me."

"I'm not stalking you. I was minding my own goddamn business, taking in the scenery." He motioned around them. "And who do I stumble over at the top? A scared little princess."

She hated when he called her princess. Alexis glared down at his knee. That hike had been tiring for her, and she wasn't carting around a leg full of scar tissue and muscle damage. "How the hell did you even get up here, anyway?"

"Same way you did—I hiked. Though I'm at least wearing appropriate clothing. What, have you never been outdoors before?"

There he went again, assuming he knew a single thing about her. She poked him in the chest, hating how defined it was. Even now, she could perfectly picture his pecs. But she wasn't going to stand here ogling him while he insulted her. "I got up here just fine."

"Sure you did. And for what? You're so scared, you're shaking like a leaf."

It stung more because he was right. Before he'd stomped up, she'd been half a second from calling the whole thing off. She couldn't do that now, not with him watching. All it would do was reinforce every shitty assumption he'd made about her. So Alexis turned around and marched to the edge of the cliff, anger propelling her even when the height made her dizzy. It was so far down, and the blue water of the fjord gleamed in the gray morning. It looked like something out of an ancient myth, carved out of the surrounding trees by some careless god. She reached the edge, and the whole world seemed to sway. "What—"

"Christ, darlin'." Luke grabbed her arm and towed her back to safety—and right against his chest. "You did it. You got to the edge."

"This is so stupid. It's not even that high. I mean, it's nearly two thousand feet. I guess that's enough. More than enough." She started shaking again, thinking about how long that drop looked. Plenty of time to think about the mistakes she'd made in life before her body hit the water with bone-crushing force.

His grip gentled on her, but his voice was just as gruff as ever. "Two thousand feet is plenty scary. Scarier than thirteen thousand feet, strangely enough. At least at the higher elevation, you know you'll have time to pull your parachute and pick a spot to land."

She looked up, hating how being close to him drove away some of the cold from her body. She wished she could blame it on memories from Cork, but it would be a lie. It was just Luke—gruff and blond and larger than life. "You'll notice I don't make a habit of jumping out of planes."

Oh my God, he's trying to make me feel better. She

thought back over the last few minutes and the shock nearly dropped her. *He's been doing it since he walked up. He goaded me to the edge, because he knew being pissed at him would distract me from being scared.*

"Your loss. It's a rush like you wouldn't believe." Something came into his voice, something a lot like longing. It made her wonder if he'd been skydiving since his injury… Which was none of her damn business.

Alexis shook her head. It was great that he'd helped her out, and her heart ached from the longing she could hear in his voice when he talked about jumping out of a plane—as insane as she found *that*—but it didn't change anything. He was here, and that was an awfully big coincidence. "How did you find me?"

His frowned at her, looking genuinely confused.

But come on, the same time, same place. Europe wasn't *that* small. "Luke, how did you find me?" She'd left him sleeping soundly, but he could've woken up and followed her to the airport. She didn't know whether to be thrilled or appalled at the thought of him, well, stalking her.

He snorted, his next words throwing that assumption right out the window. "Why the hell would I go looking for you? Don't get me wrong, the sex was amazing—"

Good Lord. "Will you please lower your voice?" She looked around, but neither of the other two groups of people seemed to be paying them the least bit of attention. *Maybe I'm just being paranoid? He's right. The sex was amazing, but it's not like he had any way to track me down, even if he wanted to.* It was just a coincidence straight out of some romantic comedy movie… If romantic comedies were populated by cranky asshole ex-military types.

No, she was looking too much into this. It might seem too convenient to believe, but he was right. What reason would he have to follow her?

"Why, princess? Am I offending your delicate sensibilities?" He gave a wicked grin that told her just how much he liked the thought. "You didn't seem that offended when my tongue was between your thighs and you were riding my mouth as you screamed my name."

"Just *shut up*." Because it was all too easy to remember exactly how good it felt when he had his mouth on her countless times the night before last.

"Don't worry your pretty head about it. It's just a strange coincidence that I'm here the same time as you." Luke finally seemed to realize he still had his arms around her, because he let go and took a step back. "Though maybe I *should* be following you. You don't seem to have the sense God gave a toddler."

Ouch. She wasn't sure what hurt more—that he thought so little of her, or that he could dismiss the sex they'd had in a few short sentences. She might have left him yesterday morning, but that had nothing to do with him or the sex.

She hated how dismissive he was of everything about her, and so she spoke without thinking. "And you do?" She sent a pointed look at his knee. "I'm not the only one shaking." A low blow, and one she instantly regretted. *You're a goddam nurse, and you're poking at his injury because he pissed you off. Classy, Alexis. Really classy.*

As he started to say something, the skies opened up. Luke cursed, but she only tipped her face up and breathed out some of her anger. If she'd wanted to bicker with someone, she could have stayed at home and gone head-to-head with Drew or even Ryan. This trip was bigger than some grouchy former military man who seemed determined to make her life a thousand times more difficult.

Her peace lasted all of ten seconds, when her body registered that she was soaked and the cold set in. Alexis wrapped her arms around herself and looked around. Both the other groups were hustling back down the way they'd come, huddled inside Windbreakers and their packs. Not Luke, though. Of course she wouldn't be that lucky. He just stood there, glowering at her. "What? Don't you have some other helpless woman to bully?"

Unexpectedly, he laughed. The sound rolled through her, deep and addicting. *Oh my God.* Luke shook his head. "Bullying you is a full-time job." He seemed to consider for a second. "And you're anything but helpless, even if you are a giant pain in my ass."

Once again, she was struck that his crappy attitude seemed calculated to keep her distracted from the huge drop just a few feet away. She wasn't sure if she should thank him or smack him for interfering in the first place—even if he *did* help get her to the edge. "Was that an actual compliment? I might pass out right here from the shock."

"Princess, if you're passing out from anything, it'll be hypothermia." He eyed her backpack. "Did it cross that pretty little head of yours to put on a fucking jacket before you traipsed through Norway?"

Wow, he was really doling out the backhanded compliments today. She glared. "I had a jacket, which I took off when I got too warm." She wasn't a complete idiot. Maybe her clothing choices didn't line up with what he thought was smart, but she had come prepared. Mostly.

"You're not too warm now."

She followed his gaze down and nearly groaned when she saw her nipples, very present and accounted for, pressing against the thin fabric of her sundress. Determined not to give him the satisfaction of showing how uncomfortable she was, she lifted her chin…and was instantly caught in his sea-green eyes.

Chapter Eight

Luke was about to demand that Alexis put her damn jacket back on when she kissed him. He should hustle her back to the hotel and get her properly clothed before she ended up sick, but all he did was pull her closer and kiss her back. It was even better than last time, her tongue stroking along his and tasting like peppermint. Alexis dropped her pack and leaned fully against him, her breasts pressing against his chest. He gave in to the need to reach down and cup her ass under her dress, and he nearly went to his knees when he found her wearing another thong. "If I'd hiked up here behind you, we never would have made it."

She laughed against his mouth. "Hmm? Maybe that's why those guys never passed me on the trail."

Jealousy hit him, even more potent than their first night together. He wound his hand through her hair, forcing her head back so she had to look at him. "You flashed a little extra ass at them on purpose, didn't you?"

Her hazel eyes were defiant. “Even bent over at the waist to tie my boots once or twice.”

The thought of those nameless men staring at her perfect ass—at any of her—made Luke see red. A rational part of his mind pointed out that she was likely just goading him, the same way she had with the soccer players, which gave him pause for half a second before a wicked thought occurred. *Two can play that game*. “You want to give some stranger a show?”

He cast a quick look around the cliff, but everyone else had cleared out, leaving them alone. Satisfied there was no one else here to see, he reached up and pushed one strap of her dress off her shoulder. The wet fabric clung to her breast, and so he was forced to give it another tug. The white bra was soaked through, revealing a clear outline of her nipple, but he didn't give in to the temptation to suck her there. Instead, he met her gaze as he pulled the lace down to bare her. “We can do that.”

Her chest rose and fell with each harsh breath, and she arched her back, pressing her breast into his hand. “There you go again—all talk and no walk.”

“You can push all you want. I'm doing this in my own time.”

“And if I say no?”

He stopped his meandering path up her side and met her gaze. “Are you saying no?”

She licked her lips, and her body shook as a shiver overtook her. He wished he could chalk it up to lust, but the ugly truth was they were standing outside in cold rain and she wasn't even close to properly dressed. He'd have to be some kind of dick to push her when there was a very real risk of hypothermia if they didn't get moving and to shelter. Cursing, Luke pulled her bra up and fixed her dress. Then he made himself let go of her and step back. Strangely enough, that was even more difficult than covering up the nipple begging for his mouth.

Alexis frowned. "I didn't say no. Hell, I'm half a second away from screaming *yes, yes, yes*. Who's getting cold feet now?"

"Both of us." He motioned at the sky. "If you still want it, I'm more than happy to spend a few hours warming you up with my mouth—but not until we get off this godforsaken cliff. Where are you staying?"

She seemed to consider not answering, but then she let out a shuddering breath. "The lodge in Jørpeland. I took the bus here."

"It's your lucky day, then. I rented a car." He'd driven in from Stavanger since he had no idea where she was. At least she was closer.

"My lucky day? That remains to be seen." Without another word, she marched off in the direction of the path.

All Luke really wanted to do was sit down and rest his damn knee, but he followed her anyway. He'd lived through worse pain, with a shittier end result. Alexis, in bed again. Even as he struggled down the boulders, keeping an eye on her in case she got cocky and fell as a result, he couldn't help wondering if this was one hell of a mistake.

One night could be called a moment of insanity, brought on by adrenaline, snarky commentary, and a convenient bar brawl. Once he'd kissed her and she'd thrown down her challenge, the end result was all but written on the wall. To do it a second time… That was damn near premeditated. He was supposed to be protecting her, not bending her in half and fucking her into submission.

Though *that* was a thought. Maybe if he kept her exhausted from constant sex, she'd be too drained to take off without him again.

Luke shook his head, breathing hard as he dropped off the last boulder and to the relatively flat ground. It was only the first in a long descent, but he felt as if he'd really accomplished something. Then Alexis glanced back, a small line between her brows. "Are you okay? We can stop for a few minutes if you need it."

She thought he was weak. Weak enough that she was offering him an easy out. There wasn't exactly pity on her face, but the compassion was only a step away. He'd seen it too many times over the last couple years, and having it appear on her face was the last thing he wanted. "I don't need a break."

He shouldered past her and picked up his pace, even though his knee screamed at the strain. It didn't matter. He wasn't weak. He refused to be. All that mattered was getting to the bottom of this fucking mountain and shoving Alexis in a room so she wouldn't wander off while he had a chance to recover. She could shove her pity while she was at it.

"With that permanent thundercloud you have hanging around your ears, it's no wonder it's raining."

"Life's not all rainbows and sunshine, princess. The sooner you figure that out, the better." He'd known that ever since he was a kid, when Aunt Rose had to step in because his deadbeat mother bounced out and left him to fend for himself at the tender age of seven. That truth was only reinforced as he grew up and joined the Air Force, where he had the pleasure of witnessing firsthand the horrible shit that people did to one another in wartime. The truth was that life wasn't pretty or clean or neat. It was a goddamn mess.

She made a pissed-off hissing sound. "For the last time, you don't know a single thing about me. So take your bad attitude and shove it up your ass."

She was right. He, of all people, shouldn't be judging the hell out of her without hearing her story. He knew that, but it was so goddamn hard to focus when his instincts were all fucked up when it came to this woman. Part of him—a very large part—wanted to protect her, even though it was obviously the last thing *she* wanted. The other part of him blamed her for prying him out of his comfortable misery back home. He knew that holing up in Aunt Rose's basement wasn't a legit life decision—in fact, he was pretty sure she was less than a month from kicking his ass to the curb in her usual tough-love style—but it had been comfortable. Now, because of Alexis, he was in fucking Norway, hiking down a cliff where each step was agony.

It wasn't her fault. Not really. But he needed his anger to get through the next few hours, so he wrapped it around himself and used it to propel him down the mountain path. A little longer. Just a little long and he could rest.

If looks could kill, Alexis would have drilled a hole in the back of Luke's head by now. He really thought he had her number down. Princess, he called her, as if the worst crisis she'd ever had to deal with was a bad hair day. The outside of her body might not be marked up, but her scars would give his a run for his money. Not that she was about to enlighten him. She'd come here to put that part of her life behind her, not dredge it up to prove to some asshole that she was worth a damn.

She was more than the cancer that had demanded the removal of her ability to have kids as penance for her life. It didn't win. *She* did. Even though she came out of that year feeling like she was walking off a battlefield into a strange version of the reality she'd once known. She wasn't going to wave that knowledge in front of him. Pity wasn't something she wanted—especially not from him—and she didn't want him to start treating her with kid gloves like so many other people in her life.

But maybe he could stand to be a little less of a grumpy ass.

By the time they made it to the bottom of the path, she simultaneously wanted to kick him in the shin and offer him a shoulder to lean on. He didn't seem to notice he was weaving on his feet, but she half expected him to topple at any second. God, this was the last thing she needed. The man was so much easier to deal with when he ran his mouth and acted like a dick.

Either way, he favored his right leg so much, there was no way he could drive. *Elevation and ice is what he needs. Probably some ibuprofen, too, if we can find it.* He wasn't the type to accept help, even from a registered nurse, but that was too damn bad. Crappy attitude or not, he'd gotten her to the edge of that cliff, and so she was going to do what she could to help his pain.

She picked up her pace as he pulled a set of keys from his pocket. Alexis grabbed them out of his hand and danced back when he turned on her. He'd already proven that he didn't want her pity—which she understood all too well—so she'd take a page from his handbook and snarl him into submission. Putting as much snark into her voice as possible, she said, "I know where we're going, so I'm driving. End of story."

For a second, she thought he'd argue, but Luke just shook his head. "Whatever you say, princess. Your way or the highway, right?"

She'd never been that unbending even once in her life, but she nodded all the same. The faster they got back to the lodge, the faster he could sit his ass down and rest. "That's exactly right." He should know something about that, being stubborn as all get out.

"Figures." He stomped over to a tiny red Volkswagen Golf. When she just stared, trying to reconcile this large man with the itty-bitty car, Luke glared. "It's all they had."

"I didn't say a word."

"I can read it all over your face." He marched over to the driver's side, opened the door, and then marched back to the passenger door. At her blank look, his glare only deepened. "What? My auntie raised me right. Get in the car."

Wordlessly, she rounded the front bumper, tossed her pack into the back, and slid into the driver's seat. What was she supposed to say? Alexis couldn't remember a single time a man had opened a door for her. Oh, Drew and Ryan did it from time to time, but that was different. She didn't see them as *men*. But a boyfriend? Never. Even Eric had claimed to be so enlightened that it was his firm belief that feminism meant women should open their own damn doors and pay their own checks. They'd split every single date's cost until they were engaged. And she'd patted herself on the back for not needing a man to take care of her then—or now.

That said… She liked the feeling that came when Luke opened her door, even if he was surly about it.

It was something to think about later, when she had time and space to be alone. She turned out onto the street and headed back toward the lodge where she'd spent the night last night. The drive was really pretty, the road curving through so much greenery, it was like a completely different world than back home. The man sitting beside her only added to the surreal feeling. In Wellingford, Luke never would have looked twice at her, and she never would have had the courage to push and prod and meet him every step of the way. She liked the New Alexis. She liked her a lot.

She just needed to figure out how to keep the changes when she finally went home.

The silence stretched, threatening to become uncomfortable—at least for her. He was staring out the window, and she wasn't really sure what to do with a contemplative Luke. He was so much easier to deal with when he was snapping and snarling at her. "Thank you."

"Not necessary. I do it for every woman." He spoke without looking over.

She took half a second and considered letting it go. What would it hurt for him not to realize she knew what he'd been up to on the cliff? But he was the one who got her those final steps to the edge. She had to acknowledge that, for herself if not for him. "No, I mean thanks for back there—for goading me into getting to the edge." She wasn't sure if she could have done it without anger at him driving her.

"You would have gotten there on your own eventually. I

just sped up the process."

Shock spread through her, and she tightened her grip on the wheel. He threw it out so casually, as if he had no doubt in his mind that she would have made it to the edge. Just like that. This man, who seemed barely able to stand the sight of her half the time they spent together, had more faith in her than she had in herself.

She didn't know how to respond to that, so she didn't say anything. As they wound around the lake next to the massive building, her mind turned to the promise he'd made her at the top of Preikestolen. His mouth, her body, hours lost. She shouldn't be so distracted by a man she barely knew, but if he was here through coincidence—and, really, what other logical reason would have put him at the top of that cliff at the same time as her?—the universe couldn't be more clear than if it'd put up a big sign over his head that read PAY ATTENTION TO HIM!

The problem was, she was still having a hell of a time believing that it was a coincidence. *He could be a killer who's stalking me.* Even as the thought crossed her mind, she discarded it. If he were going to murder her and wear her skin as a birthday suit, he had more than enough opportunity in Cork when she was in his room, sleeping and vulnerable. And that cliff they'd just scaled—yeah, he could've pushed her right off it.

Alexis had her plan when she hopped that white-knuckled flight out of Philadelphia, but she hadn't shared it with anyone. She'd picked a few places that had been important, either to her or to her mother. To anyone on the outside looking in, they'd be completely random and impossible to anticipate.

She'd only told…

She shot a look at him, slouched and glaring out the windshield. The only person she'd told was Avery. Surely her sister wouldn't have… Alexis nearly cursed aloud. Of course Avery would. And even if she wouldn't, Drew most certainly would. "Do you know Drew Flannery or Avery Yeung?" Even as she asked, part of her whispered *please, please, please don't be true*.

Luke yawned. "Who?" Not even so much of a twitch at their names. If he had been sent here to babysit her, surely he would have given himself away?

She didn't know. There was no way to tell for sure, but the possibility seemed less and less likely the more she thought about it. Where the hell would they have found this man, after all? She might not be as close to Drew as her sister was, but he wouldn't have just contracted some random guy. He was far too overprotective for that, and no way would Avery have stood for it. Still… "What branch of the military did you say you were part of?"

Another yawn. "Marines."

Well, that was that. Drew's brother, Ryan, was Air Force. It didn't mean he didn't have contact with Marines, but anyone he trusted enough to send after her would be someone he'd worked with—someone he trusted with his own life, let alone hers. Which obviously wasn't Luke. Honestly, she couldn't see this angry man and nice guy Ryan having a single conversation, let alone spending enough time together to create a friendship.

Thank God.

It truly was just a coincidence that he'd ended up here the same time she had. Alexis nodded to herself and turned into the parking lot of the lodge. *Good. And if I'm going in for a penny, I might as well go in for a pound.* She shut off the car and looked at him. "Don't bother booking a room. You'll be with me tonight."

Chapter Nine

After that damning proclamation, Luke should have told her to go to hell. As much as he'd wanted to strip her down up on Pulpit Rock, now he was so tired, he'd be lucky if he didn't pass out right here in the passenger seat of this tiny-ass car. But the lure of a bed and a hot shower got him moving when Alexis climbed out of the driver's seat. "Sorry, princess, I'm not really in the mood anymore."

"That's cute, but I wasn't talking about sex. I'm afraid if I leave you alone, you're going to end up unconscious and suffering from that hypothermia you were so worried about."

Right. She wasn't concerned with getting him naked—she just wanted to make sure his weak ass didn't hurt himself. "In the immortal words of Princess Alexis—I can take care of myself."

She glanced over her shoulder long enough to glare at him. "Could you tone down on the caveman charm for a few minutes? You're going to scare the villagers, and then we'll be dealing with torches and pitchforks."

Like they'd gone after Frankenstein. "You have no idea how accurate that description is." Most days he felt like he'd been pieced together, his body no longer his own. There wasn't a mad doctor waiting in the wings, laughing maniacally, though. It was just him, a prisoner crippled by his boatload of issues.

They walked through the lobby, and she led the way deeper into the lodge. "You're right. Poor, scarred Luke. Nobody understands him."

"Are you *mocking* me?" He'd spent weeks in a hospital being put back together, followed by months of physical therapy—not to mention the loss of his career, identity, and most of his friends. That wasn't something to poke fun at. He was still trying to find his feet after everything he'd lost.

"Not what happened to you." She stopped in front of a door and opened it, standing back to let him limp in. He had a second to thank God it was a single occupancy instead of the bunk setup, and then Alexis kept going, "But seriously, could you be any more tortured about it? I've seen men who lost all their limbs who still managed to have a better attitude than you do."

"You don't get it." His entire identity had been tied up in the pararescuers. He was the man all the badasses in the armed forces called when they needed help. He saved lives and ran headlong into situations that would send most people fleeing scared, and he'd loved every second of it.

That was all beyond his reach now, gone in a split second.

"You're right. I don't. I'm sure there isn't another person in this world who's been hurt like you have." She rolled her eyes. "Whatever you have to tell yourself to sleep at night, Luke. Every single person has lost something and some of us..." Her voice broke, surprising him so much that he dropped into the single chair. "Some of us have actually lost *everything*."

What the hell was he supposed to say to that? That nothing in her perfect princess life could measure up to his crawling back from the brink of death? Saying as much suddenly felt on the far side of crass. There was something in her eyes, something that called to him on a foundational level. She looked like a woman who'd walked through hell and back, just the same as he had. *What the hell happened to you, darlin'?* "Alexis—"

"Forget it." She headed for the door. "I'm going to go find the laundry room and see about some ice for your knee. Why don't you lay your stuff out and give it a chance to dry?"

Before he could formulate a response, she was gone, shutting the door behind her. Luke closed his eyes and leaned back to smack his head on the wall a few times. It didn't do anything for the toxic mix of lust and anger inside him. So he decided to do something useful and dry out his shit. The two pairs of jeans he had were filthy from all the goddamn walking, and his shirts weren't in much better condition. Doing laundry had just become the number one priority.

Not wanting to waste this opportunity, he grabbed his satellite phone and dialed. As expected, Flannery picked up on the second ring. "Yeah?"

"I found her."

A sigh of relief. "Thank God. Avery is losing her shit over this whole thing. Drew is convinced it's going to mess with the baby, and no one can convince him otherwise."

"Well, she didn't fall to her death from a drop of two thousand feet, so that should reassure everyone." He paused, making sure there was no sound of footsteps on the other side of the door. "She's fine. A huge pain in my ass, but fine."

"Good. You've got to keep up with her, man."

"I'm trying. At some point, if I keep showing up where she is, she's going to either call the cops or figure out something's up." And he didn't relish the conversation either of those options would bring about.

"Convince her to bring you along. She can't know that we didn't trust her to do this alone." Another sigh. "She needs this, Jacks."

Even hearing his old PJ nickname wasn't enough to distract him. She needed to have everyone at home so torn up and worried that her pregnant sister was possibly endangering her unborn kid? For the millionth time, he wondered what the hell she'd gone through to make everyone so willing to let her jaunt off to find herself. He could ask Flannery, and it was likely the man would even tell him, but Luke held off.

He wanted to hear it from her.

He cleared his throat. "If Avery's so worried, why don't I just pack her up and bring her home?"

"No. Stick with the plan."

That's what he thought his former squad mate would say. For the first time since he agreed to this insane mission, he was actually grateful. Getting Alexis to agree to his tagging along was going to be a chore, but part of him relished the challenge. She didn't give an inch, and as frustrating as he found that sometimes, he actually admired that part of her. It made him want to know more, even though getting any closer to her was a goddamn mistake. "Roger that."

"Thanks, man. I…know this can't be easy on you."

"I'm fine." And he sure as hell didn't need to be coddled. "I'll keep you updated." He hung up before Flannery could say anything else to insinuate that he wasn't up to par. It wasn't intentional, but that didn't make it sting any less. The sad truth was that he *wasn't* in fighting shape anymore. Nothing anyone did or said was going to change that.

Footsteps sounded in the hallway as he stuffed the phone back into his pack and dumped his dirty clothes onto the floor. She'd been right to figure out the laundry situation first. God alone knew where they were headed next. He didn't relish the thought of walking around, smelling like several-day-old clothing.

Alexis opened the door and paused, her gaze going to the pile of clothes. "I found the laundry room." She held up a plastic bucket. "And ice."

He grabbed his last clean pair of boxer briefs and stripped down, ignoring Alexis's shocked exhale. He might have no interest in jumping her bones right now—which was a dirty lie with her standing there, her wet dress clinging to her body until she somehow looked more sensual than if she were naked—but he was done hiding from her. If she turned away from his scars now, after what they'd done the other night, then she would only confirm everything he was so sure of when it came to her.

And if she *didn't* turn away…

Alexis couldn't move as Luke kicked off his pants. After how careful he'd been to make sure she didn't see his scars the other night, he was stripping in front of her. One look at the angry challenge in his eyes and she understood. He thought she was going to shy away or flinch, and it was easier to go on the attack than to take it passively. Well, tough luck. Everyone had scars—his just happened to be physical, in addition to the mental load he so obviously carried around.

She was the last person who was going to falter when it came to other people's issues. She had far too many of her own.

When he was finally naked in front of her, she let herself look her fill. God, he was magnificent. The scars only added to the picture, winding up his right leg and side, drawing attention to his narrow waist, leading up to a set of pectoral muscles that made her mouth water. Even his half-finished tattoo sleeves only created a picture of a man who was in the midst of change.

Kind of like her.

It wasn't a comfortable realization, because it made her feel closer to him, and if his actions over the last few days were anything to go by, he didn't *want* anyone closer to him. What were the odds that she'd go to Europe and end up spending time with a man who was just as broken as she was?

Luke held out his hands, as if asking, *Well?*

She shrugged. "I've seen worse."

He blinked, the shock on his face almost hilarious. She knew better than to laugh, though. Who was the last person he let see him like this? *I bet it was someone he was in love with. I bet whoever she was, she flinched away from him and added yet another scar to the mix*. It was enough to make her wish she had the ability to reach back through history and slap the shit out of whoever she was—and Alexis had no doubt it was a woman. This level of almost-insecurity didn't come from comments made from the same sex.

As they stood there, staring at each other, she had to do something to break the moment. It felt too fragile, too intimate. She couldn't fix Luke. She couldn't even fix herself. But maybe she could ensure that he walked away from their time together with a few experiences to mark in the "good" column.

After all, he'd already done the same for her.

Alexis held up the bucket of ice. "Why don't you go shower and then put some ice on that knee? I'll get the laundry started."

"Laundry. Right." With a nod, he disappeared into the bathroom and shut the door. A few seconds later, the shower started.

Then, and only then, did she slouch to the bed and let out the breath she hadn't realized she'd been holding. She'd known Luke was as damaged—like called to like—but somehow this new realization hit harder than that basic knowledge. Someone had hurt him, beyond the devastating physical injury. With each new piece of information she carved away, she was forced to face the facts—they weren't nearly as different as she'd thought. If he didn't think she was so damn worthless, they might have even…

Alexis laughed. Might have what? Fallen into a bed of roses and used their mutual understanding to heal each other's brokenness? That kind of thing only happened in movies. The reality was that each person had to look inside themself for the strength to move past their issues. No one else could make that decision for someone else.

Life might be so much easier if they *could*.

Shaking her head, she emptied her dirty clothes onto the pile with his and set aside a pair of yoga pants and a tank top for later. It took ten minutes to stuff everything in and start the machine, and by the time she made it back to the room, Luke was sprawled on the tiny bed in just his underwear, a makeshift ice pack on his knee. The sight of him sent things low in her stomach tightening, and she stopped inside the doorway, not sure what to do about it. Her first impulse was to crawl into bed with him and use her mouth to explore every inch of exposed skin, but he needed to rest more than she needed his hands on her body.

She had no idea what to do with the protective urge that rose inside her. He didn't want her help. He'd probably snap at her if she even tried.

He's using the ice, which means he's in more pain that he wants to admit.

There wasn't much she could do for an old injury. Alexis wasn't a surgical nurse, and even if she were, he'd healed. Now it was a matter of him coming to terms with his new limits and doing the best he could not to injure the weakened knee worse. She had a feeling he was having a hell of a time with both those things.

Alexis dug through her bag to find the bottle of ibuprofen she'd stashed in a side pocket and tapped out two pills. "Take these."

"I'm not your patient." But he still took the pills and dry-swallowed them. "You don't have to baby me."

"I'm not. And admitting that you overdid it doesn't mean you're failing." She didn't look at him as she spoke, concentrating on reorganizing her bag. She had the strangest feeling like she was approaching a wild creature that was as likely to take off her arm as it was to run away. It wasn't that she wanted Luke to pour out his heart to her… Not really.

To distract both of them, she said, "What do you do for work?"

He snorted. "Nice change of subject."

God, he was so prickly. Alexis looked up long enough to shoot him a glare. "Yeah, well, you obviously don't want to talk about your knee, and sitting here in silence isn't my idea of a good time."

"Okay, I'll play. Right now I'm helping out at my cousin's shop. Basically, if it's American made, he can fix it. Even if it's not, he can probably fix it." His voice dropped so low she almost missed the next part. "Don't need two good legs to work on cars."

She set her bag to the side. "Or a good attitude, either."

Luke scowled. "I lost everything when that IED took me out. Maybe I'm not clasping my hands and singing 'Kumbaya' around a campfire, but I still manage to get out of bed every morning without putting a gun in my mouth and ending it all."

"Is that really an option you've considered?" The thought of the world without him in it made her stomach lurch, but she kept her tone quiet and steady.

"No, damn it." He didn't look the least bit happy to admit it, either. "I lived. For whatever reason, my time came and went on that operating table, and I'm still kicking." He took a sharp breath and seemed to struggle to rein in his temper. "I know I'm a mean bastard, and I know it doesn't seem like it some days, but I *am* happy to be alive."

She watched the truth dawn on his face, and wondered if this was the first time he'd said as much aloud. "Good." She wanted to say more, to point out that there was so much more to the world than war and death and loss, but with her own loss like a monkey on her back, it felt hypocritical in the extreme. Luke admitted he was happy to be alive. That was as much a step in the right direction as her journey to the top of Pulpit Rock earlier.

I won't be there to see the end of it.

The truth settled in her chest, as heavy as a boulder. Maybe he was in Europe for the same reason she was, but their time would come to an end and their paths would split, and she'd never see the moment he let the chains of the past go. Because he would. She was suddenly sure of that.

"What happened to you?"

Alexis looked up and froze, a deer facing off with a hungry wolf. The way Luke's eyes pinned her in place certainly felt predatory. "What?"

"Give me a little credit here, darlin'. You didn't just decide to travel by yourself through Europe for no reason. Well-adjusted people don't feel the need to hike to the top of a cliff and touch the edge. Trust me." He jerked a thumb at his chest. "It takes one to know one."

This was the moment. He'd bared his physical scars to her. Now she had the choice between returning the favor with her emotional scars or turning away. She opened her mouth, but the words wouldn't come. There were too many other voices in her head. Eric's saying, "You weren't that much of a catch to begin with, Alexis. And now I'm expected to give up my future children? Absolutely not." *Yé-yé's* saying, "You had *one job*, and you've failed at that, Alexis. You bring shame on our family." On her dark days, she suspected they both would have been happier if the cancer took her life, instead of her uterus. Even her sister's saying, "I'm pregnant." All of them reminders of how she'd dropped the ball as a woman.

She couldn't stand the thought of seeing the same disappointment reflected in Luke's sea-green eyes. He might find her aggravating as all get out, but he *wanted* her. Would he still feel the same way if he knew about the cancer?

I can't take that chance.

She pushed to her feet. "I need a shower."

"Ah, hell, princess. Just when I thought we were getting somewhere."

Shame heated the back of her neck as she slipped into the bathroom and shut the door, but it wasn't enough to make her stop and turn around and pour out her broken heart to him.

Chapter Ten

Call him a fool, but Luke was actually surprised when Alexis basically dived into the bathroom to escape him. He wished his question had been idle curiosity—it would have made her retreat easier to bear—but his need to know more about her past had taken on a life of its own. She was so damn strong in so many ways. Aggravating as hell sometimes, but strong. She'd looked at his scars and then called him out.

Even his Aunt Rose had reacted at the sight of his knee. She'd gone back to the ball-busting woman he knew almost immediately afterward, but that half a second of horror on her face had been enough to confirm what he'd already known. He was fucked up beyond repair.

And then here came this little woman who seemed to have more stubbornness than common sense to shine a light on him in a way he'd never experienced before. Alexis didn't look at him and see a broken man, never able to be whole again. She acknowledged his injury the same way she'd acknowledge that he had green eyes or blond hair—just a part of him, no greater or smaller than any other part.

He didn't know what the hell he was supposed to do about that.

A scream brought him to his feet before he registered the decision to move. A second one had him hurtling through the bathroom door, ignoring the protest his knee made. He found Alexis huddled in the corner of the shower, but after a quick glance to make sure she wasn't hurt, he bypassed her to search for the threat.

"What's wrong? Why'd you scream?" He turned in another circle, wondering what the hell he'd missed. Unlike a lot of the rooms in hostels scattered around Europe, this one had its own private bathroom, which meant there was no way for anyone else to gain access to it without coming into the room itself. Luke might have been distracted, but he sure as hell would have seen someone walk by him.

The room was empty except for her.

She pointed a shaking finger, and he followed the line down to the… He blinked, part of him wondering if this was some kind of joke. "A spider. You screamed bloody murder because of a tiny half-drowned spider."

Alexis made another frightened noise that was just this side of a shriek. "Kill it. Oh my God, *just kill it.*"

Even though she was obviously afraid, he couldn't help a little snark. "Don't move. I think it can smell fear." He hurried back into the bedroom and retrieved a boot. One well-placed smash later, the threat was eliminated—and his boot was wet. "He's gone. You're safe."

"Thanks." She looked around the bathroom as if

expecting more spiders to pour from the vents or something.

Luke shook his head, not sure if he should hug her or laugh his ass off. "Princess, you kicked my ass and laughed at me afterward. You scaled a twenty-story cliff. How are you possibly afraid of a little bug?"

Her shiver was so violent, it made the rings on the shower curtain rattle. "You're a grown man. Grown men do not *scuttle*." She shuddered. "Spiders scuttle. It's freaky and unnatural."

Holy shit, she was downright precious. He grinned. "The distinction is noted." And so were the soapsuds sliding down from her hair, between her breasts, and over the long line of her stomach. He wanted to trace that same path with his tongue, and take it one step further to drape her leg over his shoulder so he had nothing stopping his ability to taste her there.

Suddenly, he wasn't feeling all that tired at all.

"If you could see the way you're looking at me."

"Like what?" He already knew. He just wanted to hear her say it. He didn't think he'd ever get tired of hearing filthy words come out of Alexis Yeung's mouth.

She licked her lips. "Like you want to take me up against this shower wall."

Christ, but he did. Luke didn't say anything, though. Not yet. He just let himself look his fill, tracing her body with his gaze, from her pale pink toenails to her long legs, the tempting vee between her thighs, her nipples that practically begged for his mouth, and finally to her challenging hazel eyes. She was the most perfectly shaped woman he'd ever seen, and the fire of her personality only made her more attractive.

"Are you going to stand there and stare or are you going to lose the underwear and join me?" The tone of her voice said she didn't think it was much of a decision, and she was right.

But there was one thing they needed to cover first. "The conversation isn't over between us."

"I'm sorry?"

She knew exactly what he was talking about. He could read the knowledge all over her wide eyes and the way her body shook. "You will tell me about your past, and what happened to you. Eventually." As much as he wanted to have the information right this second, it wouldn't mean a damn thing if he forced it out of her. He wanted her to *want* to tell him. "When you're ready."

"And if I'm never ready?"

That was the question, wasn't it? This thing between them had an expiration date, something he'd do damn well to remember. Luke met her gaze, seeing far more than he knew she'd want him to. *Damn, darlin', you have scars to rival mine, don't you?* "You will be."

"You seem so sure. I wish I could be that sure." She glanced away and then back, resolve showing in her expression. "Why are you still wearing underwear?"

He let the previous subject go. Sex was easy, and with how scraped raw he felt right now, it was exactly what he needed—what they both needed.

"Good question." He shucked off the boxer briefs and paused. Condom. Under no circumstances was he giving either of them a reason to put this thing on pause again. "Five seconds."

"One." She held up a finger. "Two."

Luke practically dived for her pack, riffling through it and dumping things to the side until he came up with a string of condoms. He ripped one open and had it rolled on by the time he stepped back through the bathroom door. Alexis had her eyes closed and head tipped back under the spray of water as she rinsed the shampoo from her hair. He was almost—almost—reluctant to step in and ruin the look of peace on her face.

Then she opened her eyes and held out her hand, silently commanding him to get the hell in there. *My pleasure, darlin'.* He took her hand and stepped into the spray of water, using the move to pull her into his arms. She pressed against the front of his body and turned them around until he was backed against the chilled tile. Then she went onto her tiptoes and kissed him, her tongue darting into his mouth. He groaned against her lips and palmed her ass, bringing her flush against the hard length of his cock.

"Take me, Luke."

As if he planned on doing anything else. He turned her around and reached between her thighs and stroked her, fucking her slowly with his finger, making both of them wait for what they really wanted. "You want me here." He added a second finger, nearly moaning when she clenched around him.

"I want you right there." She spread her legs a little more and leaned back against his chest, giving him full access to her body. "I want you so deep, I won't know where I end and you begin." She gasped when he cupped her breast and rolled her nipple between his fingers. "I want you to make me come."

"Your wish is my command." He briefly considered and

discarded pinning her against the shower wall. With his bum knee, it was an emergency room visit just waiting to happen.

Instead, he maneuvered her to the back of the shower, pressing a hand between her shoulder blades until she bent over and braced herself on the wall. He stroked her again, using his fingers to spread her wetness up and around her clit. She moaned, arching back into him, tilting her hips to offer herself. "Hold still, darlin'."

He positioned his cock at her entrance and pushed inside with one smooth movement. They both froze, though her body shook beneath his hands. Luke gritted his teeth and forced himself to hold still, even though he needed to thrust, to pound into her.

But then she pulled away and shoved herself against him. "More. I need more."

He gripped her hips, keeping her from doing that again. "Darlin'—"

"*Now*, Luke."

This time, when she pushed back, he met her halfway. He tightened his hold on her hips, helping her move against him, filling her completely. "You love this, don't you? You love the way I fuck you."

"Yes. Oh my God, yes."

"Touch yourself. Reach between your legs and rub your clit for me." When she obeyed, a shudder racked her body and she tightened around him. "That's right. Just like you like it."

"Harder."

He shoved into her hard enough to have her scrambling for purchase on the tile wall. "Like this. This is what you want."

"Oh, yes." Her head dropped forward, her hair parting to reveal the long line of her back. As much as he wanted to lick his way down her spine, he was too focused on holding off long enough to push her over the edge.

Changing his angle, he pulled her up, bending her backward to claim a kiss. While his tongue thrust against hers, he pushed her hand out of the way and stroked her clit. "I'm the only one allowed to make you come, darlin'. Me and no one else." He rolled his hips, pushing deeper. "Tell me."

Her breath sobbed out. "You, Luke. You're the only one who makes me come like this."

"Don't you dare forget it." The possessive feeling had no place here, but he couldn't shake it. Especially when she cried out his name as she came. How the hell was he supposed to keep his distance with her milking his cock like this?

The answer was swept away as his orgasm exploded through him. He held her tightly enough to bruise as the last of his strength went out of his legs. They wobbled, but Alexis caught the wall and steadied them. "Wow."

Wow was right. He wasn't sure there were words to describe what they'd just done—or the fact that he wanted it again as soon as possible. It didn't make any sense. He'd had relationships in the past, but he'd never felt this level of sheer… Christ, he didn't know what to call it. Lust. Desire. *Need.*

He pressed a kiss to the back of her neck and straightened. Words rose, words he didn't know what to do with. Alexis kept giving him intriguing glimpses of a woman who wasn't anything like he'd expected. He didn't know how he was supposed to respond. Or if he even should.

She'll never forgive me if she found out why I'm really here.

Now wasn't the time or place for those thoughts, so he put them out of his head and got rid of the condom. By the time Alexis turned around, he'd rinsed off. She gave him a dazed smile. "Wow again."

He wanted to stay in the shower, soap up his hands, and use washing her as an excuse to explore her body. Because he wanted it so desperately, he kissed her and stepped back. But that didn't stop six treacherous words from slipping free. "I can't get enough of you."

This thing already had an expiration date, even if she didn't find out that her sister and friends had sent him over here to look after her. A few days. A week, maybe a little more. As long as it took for her to find what she was looking for and go back to her life.

Her smile was a little unsure. "I kind of feel the same way."

He couldn't afford to forget that he had a temporary role here, and that wasn't about to change. They were worlds apart. It was only a strange circumstance that brought them together right now. Hell, he was pretty damn sure he didn't even like her.

But as he dried off, he couldn't shake the feeling that he was a goddamn liar. He liked Alexis. A whole hell of a lot more than he should.

Chapter Eleven

Luke walked back into the room as Alexis dried off, and his attention snagged on the bag she'd spent time organizing—and that he'd practically dumped out in his search for condoms. He tucked the towel more firmly around his waist and sank carefully to the floor next to it. The least he could do was put things to right here.

He started putting the various things back into the empty interior pockets they'd obviously fallen out of, but stopped when something crinkled in his hand. He frowned and pulled it out of the backpack. It was a picture of a couple that he suspected were Alexis's parents.

"*Put it down.*"

Though every instinct demanded he drop it at the frantic tone in her voice, he lifted it up for a closer look. A Chinese man and a willowy brunette in their mid-thirties stood in front of a gazebo that looked strangely familiar. Where the hell had he seen that gazebo before? "Are these your parents?" They had to be.

"I swear to God, if you don't drop that right now, I'm going to hurt you."

Luke finally looked up to find her in the doorway, pale and shaking. He could understand if she was pissed because he was theoretically going through her things—even if that wasn't his intention—but this reaction seemed extreme. "Why are you freaking out?" He knew her and Avery's mother had died quite a while ago, but that still didn't explain it.

Instead of answering, her bottom lip quivered. "Please put it down."

Holy shit, she was about to cry. He carefully set the photo down on top of her backpack and moved away when she hurried over to snatch it up. Only when it was in her hands did she take a shuddering breath and seem to get a hold of herself. "Sorry."

Did this have something to do with the shit she wasn't telling him? He resisted the urge to demand answers, and leaned back against the bed, watching her. She looked so fragile right now, like a sharp word would shatter her into a million pieces. "Care to explain?"

"It's..." Another deep breath. "It's my last photo of my parents together. Or the last one where Mom is healthy and smiling and not ravaged by cancer and chemo." Her half smile didn't come close to reaching her eyes. "When she was diagnosed, they decided to take a trip to Austria and kind of see her heritage—our heritage, I guess. This was from the *Sound of Music* tour she made Dad take." This time her smile was a little more real. "It was one of our favorite movies, and the first one I remember watching with her."

The sheer amount of loss on her face struck him dumb. There was nothing he could say to fix it, or even understand. His deadbeat mother had taken off when he was a kid, but he'd had Aunt Rose. She was as steady as the Mississippi and healthy as a horse. Luke wasn't always easy on her—even now—but he couldn't imagine a life where she was gone. "I'm sorry."

"It was a long time ago."

Maybe, but her feelings about the whole thing obviously hadn't faded over the years. Even though he'd promised himself that he wouldn't pry until she was ready, he couldn't help asking, "Is that why you're over here? Because of your mother?"

"Partly." Alexis wiped at her eyes, and because she was trying so hard to pretend there weren't tears there, he followed her lead. She tucked the picture back into her bag. "My mother was so strong and in love with life, all the way up to the end. Some people go through cancer treatments and become bitter and angry, but not her. If she could hold on to that happiness even when she knew she wasn't going to make it, it kind of puts a lot of things into perspective, you know? I should be able to do the same thing."

"*What*—"

"I'm not dying." She gave him a half smile. "But I used to be a lot more like her, and in the last few years, I've let… stuff…weigh me down until it felt like I was underwater. So I'm reclaiming myself, a little piece at a time, with the added bonus of feeling closer to her."

She might not be pouring her heart out to him, but she was giving him a glimpse of what she'd been thinking coming over here. And hell, he'd judged her too quickly. If Aunt

Rose died, wouldn't he want to hold her memory close in any way he could? It wouldn't require a trip halfway across the world, but this journey wasn't his. It was Alexis's. "So, Cork?"

"When my sister and I were little, my mom used to read us Irish fairy tales. It might seem kind of silly now, but with the way she told them, it was hard not to believe in magic and faeries and good-luck charms." She pulled her hair over her shoulder and absently started braiding it. "The Blarney Stone, in particular, always fascinated me. I've always wanted to be able to speak up and say the right thing in any given moment. It's not one of my skills."

Luke snorted. "You could have fooled me." When she frowned, he said, "Darlin', you've been speaking up and putting me in my place since the day we met."

"That's different. *You're* different."

"Or maybe you're not giving yourself enough credit." He moved on before she could argue with him. "And the cliff?"

"My mom wasn't afraid of anything." She shrugged. "There were probably simpler ways of going about it, but I stumbled across a picture of Pulpit Rock last year, and even that was enough to lock me up in fear. I made it my screen saver. I promised myself I'd go there one day, climb it, and touch the edge."

God, this woman was amazing. She'd systematically picked out parts of herself that she found lacking and done what she felt necessary to change them. He shifted up to the bed, since the floor was hurting his knee, and considered pointing out that she'd already started conquering her demons before she'd ever gotten on a plane. "Where to next?"

She hesitated and then reached into her bag and pulled out the picture. "Here."

It made sense that she'd want to visit the last place she had evidence of her parents being healthy and happy. It made his heart ache a little. "Want some company?"

"What?"

"Well, I've always had a thing for *The Sound of Music*."

Alexis laughed. "You are such a liar."

Yeah, he was. He'd seen the movie once, under protest, and been dragged to the live play another time by his auntie. But he liked that Alexis was now grinning and the shadows were gone from her face. "You're coming across very judgmental right now."

"You'd know." She sobered. "Luke—"

It was now or never. "Look, darlin', I know I might have a funny way of showing it sometimes, but I like you. I think you're stronger than you give yourself credit for, and you're sexy as fuck." He took a deep breath, feeling curiously like he was walking on a tightrope. "I'm not ready to end this. So if you're okay with it, I'd like to come with you to Austria."

She searched his face, and he had the insane thought that now was the time to fully come clean. She'd be pissed, really pissed. She might even walk away from him for good—which was no more than he deserved.

He couldn't do it. Not yet.

Alexis finally sat back. "You know, I kind of like you, too. Most of the time."

He could hardly believe what he was hearing. He'd hoped, of course, but part of him had already resigned itself to having to chase her ass to Austria when she left him again. He'd hoped after her declaration in the shower, admitting that she couldn't get enough of him either, but that was sex. Hearing that she was starting to like him, too? It settled something in his chest and lessened the tension in his bones. He managed to keep his expression neutral, but only barely. "So that's that, then?"

"I guess so." She grinned. "Let's go to Austria."

Chapter Twelve

Alexis couldn't get off the plane fast enough. Every time she moved through the short two-hour flight, her shoulder or knee brushed against Luke and set off a chain reaction of desire through her body. After his blowing her mind seven ways to Sunday in the shower last night, he'd backed off and hadn't whispered so much as a dirty word.

It felt like the entire dynamic between them had shifted, and she wasn't sure what to do with it. Letting him tag along to Austria had been a mistake, but she couldn't shake the feeling that he was starting to understand what she wanted to accomplish with this trip. There had been something almost like respect in his eyes last night.

But she still hadn't told him the truth.

Not all of it.

It was so stupid. Luke obviously understood what it was like to lose a vital part of himself and keep on kicking. If anyone could understand what she'd gone through—and what she was trying to reclaim—it would be him.

All she had to do was open her mouth and say those damning words. *I had cancer. I beat it, but it took a bloody chunk out of me in the process. I can't have kids. Hell, there's no guarantee the cancer won't come back and finish the job at some point*. That was the difference between them. He'd battled his demons. Maybe he hadn't conquered them yet, but he would—because they were in the past.

Hers could reappear at any moment.

She couldn't live her life fearing that, though. There were no guarantees, for either the good or the bad, and she'd spent the last year missing out on all sorts of experiences because fear had been in the driver's seat.

No more.

She shouldered her backpack and headed for security, Luke matching her every step of the way. A cab would be the fastest way to the hotel, and then… Then she didn't know. It was too late in the day to try for the tour, but the thought of wandering around with him glowering beside her made her skin feel too tight. All she'd wanted when she got here was some time alone to figure her issues out, and it seemed like she'd barely gotten a moment to breathe since landing in Ireland. Nothing about this trip was going as planned.

In some ways, it had gone better. Would she have reclaimed that part of herself that made her feel so…womanly…if she hadn't run into Luke in the alley? Her transformation wasn't anywhere near finished, but it had started that night in Cork when she'd met him every step of the way and goaded him into taking her back to his room. It was a move she never would have made back home in Wellingford.

And then, in Norway, she'd gotten to the edge of the

cliff. Maybe she hadn't done it entirely on her own, but she'd made that hike without help, and Luke hadn't exactly held her hand while she took those last steps to the edge.

He'd helped. It might not make her entirely comfortable, but he'd helped.

She glanced over and realized Luke was a few steps behind her. His limp wasn't as bad as it'd been last night, but it was still more prominent than in Ireland. She slowed to match his pace, which only served to annoy him if his expression was anything to go by. "I don't need special treatment."

"It's not special treatment, and you know it." She rolled her eyes. By now, she knew that he got extra snarly when his knee was hurting him. It had nothing to do with her, and she didn't mind his grouchy attitude because the bite behind it wasn't there anymore. "We'll find some more ice at the hotel."

"I'm fine."

"No, you're stubborn. I'd bet this trip is the most exercise that knee has seen since physical therapy. It's no wonder it's bothering you."

Neither one of them said anything else through the entire cab ride and checking into the hotel—which Luke insisted on paying for. She took one look at the stubborn expression on his face and just let him have his way. After she found him some ice, she'd make a trip back down to the lobby to put her payment information in instead of his.

The only reason he was in Austria was because of her. She wasn't going to let him foot the bill, too.

He led the way up the stairs and to the room halfway down the hall. Thankfully, it had a private shower and bathroom, and even had two beds. She put her hands on her hips and stared at them. *I need to get him ice and go back to the front desk.*

But the intentions failed when faced with those plain white beds. Things with Luke had become so complicated in the last twenty-four hours. Her nerves were a strained mess, and that wasn't even getting into her emotions. She had no idea what the hell was going on there.

If she brought him the ice right now, he'd be forced to lie still and they'd end up talking. With the quiet way he accepted things last night—totally unexpected considering some of their initial conversations—it was only a matter of time before she told him the rest of the story. She couldn't stand the thought of seeing disappointment in his eyes. She might be feeling stronger and more independent, but that would bring all her progress crashing down around her. She was sure of it.

But there was another option.

She dropped her pack on the floor and turned to him. "Take off your clothes."

He gave her a long look. "Feeling twitchy, are we, princess?" She couldn't shake the feeling that he knew exactly what she was trying to do right now—create a distraction.

"Yes."

"Thought so." He nodded like she'd confessed more than a single word. And then he crossed his arms over his chest, a challenge written all over his face. "You want them off? Do it yourself, then."

Desire curled through her. A chance to fully explore his body? Like hell would she say no to that. Alexis crossed the room and pushed his backpack off his shoulders. From there it would have been simple to yank off his shirt and go for the front of his jeans. But she took her time, slipping her hands under the hem of his shirt and sliding them up his chest, raising the fabric. His breath hissed out when her fingers skimmed over his nipples, and so she paused, looking directly into his eyes as she explored just how sensitive he was. "You like that."

"Yeah." Luke's voice dropped an octave or two. "Keep going."

"Don't rush me." She pushed the fabric higher, prompting him to raise his hands so she could pull the shirt over his head. After dropping it on the floor, she went back to his shoulders, following the line of the muscle roping down his arms. So strong. She wanted to ask about the unfinished tattoo on his left arm, but held back. If he answered her questions, she'd have to answer his. She wasn't ready for that. Not yet.

Instead, she traced the tattoos winding down his right arm—a ship in the midst of a violent storm, encircled by long arms rising out of the sea. Below the surface, a kraken lurked, ready to bring the sailors to their depths and, below that, a ring of skeletons in various positions circled his forearm. It was dark and gritty and she completely empathized with the lost sailors. Sometimes there was no way out, no way to win, no way to survive.

Pushing the dark thoughts aside, she stroked her hand down his scar. He opened his mouth—no doubt to throw out a biting comment—but she pressed two fingers to his lips. "Not now." If anything, his glare deepened, but he didn't say anything as she moved down to the button at the top of his jeans.

The boots. Damn it, she'd almost forgotten.

Alexis went to her knees and quickly unlaced his boots. They looked military grade, which made sense, though she'd never noticed before now. It took some wiggling and help from Luke, but she finally got them off. Then, with her still on her knees, she looked up and met his gaze. His green eyes darkened, and she could almost hear all the things he must be fighting not to say. Sexy words that seemed to drive all the way to her soul and leave their imprint there. He made her feel like a seductress who could bring men to their knees with the least bit of effort.

There's only one man I want on his knees.

You.

Luke could barely catch his breath. In the few days he'd known her, he'd spent considerable time imagining Alexis in this position in front of him. She licked her lips and he nearly groaned. "Darlin', you're killing me."

"Not yet. But I will be." She unbuttoned his jeans and worked them down his hips, taking his boxer briefs with them, lightly dragging her nails over his skin.

He braced himself for the inevitable flinch when her hand came in contact with the worst of his scars around his knee, but she gave it a cursory glance and then nudged his legs up, one at a time, to get his pants and underwear off. Once the last of his clothes were gone, she just looked at him, stripping him bare in a way he never had been before.

Alexis gave a strange little happy sigh. "You really are beautiful."

Her words hit him in the gut. She sounded like she

meant it, and he wasn't prepared for the shock to his system. What the hell did a woman like Alexis see in a scarred and battered man like himself? Whatever it was, it made her lips curve up and her eyes shine. She ducked down and pressed her lips to his knee, backing up quickly, as if she wasn't sure of her welcome.

She'd kissed him there, where most people could barely stand to look.

Luke's heart gave a heavy thump and his body felt too hot. "Again."

"You're sure?"

He swallowed down his reflexive sharp comment. Her question was serious, and so he owed her a serious answer. "Please, darlin'. Touch me." He needed her hands on him like he needed his next breath, and he wasn't about to stand in his own way, not right now. Not when it came to Alexis.

Her smile widened. "I'd hoped you'd say that." Another kiss to his knee, and then she worked her way up the outside of his right thigh, pressing kiss after kiss to the scarred skin until she hit his hip bone. Her cheek brushed his cock, and he couldn't hold back a groan. She ran her hands up his legs to his hips. "You want me here."

This was no time for games, but he couldn't stop the words demanding to be voiced. "I want those pretty lips of yours around my cock."

Another kiss to the sensitive skin inside his hip. "Tell me more."

"I want you to put that wicked mouth to use and suck me deep, until you're sure you can't take any more. I want you to use your tongue to drive me crazy until my knees buckle and all I can think about is dragging you up my body and fucking you senseless."

She took his cock in her hand and slid her fingers up and down his length. "Is that all?"

The little tease. Luke barked out a laugh. "Darlin', if you keep it up, I'm going to skip right to the *fucking you senseless* part." His breath shuddered out when she made a fist and pumped him twice. "I changed my mind. I'm going to toss you on that bed over there and rip those jeans off so there's nothing between my mouth and your skin. I've been craving another taste of you."

"Not yet. I'm running this show, remember?" And with that, she took him in, her lips sliding along his cock and her wet mouth dragging him deeper.

Luke gave up trying to hold himself back and laced his hands in her long dark hair. "That's it, darlin'. Fuck, you make me feel so goddamn good." She rolled her tongue along the underside of his cock, nearly making his eyes cross. "Christ, Alexis." He couldn't take much more of this. Desperate for her, he used his grip on hair to pull her up and into a kiss. "I need you—right now."

"Good, because the feeling's mutual." She pulled her shirt off while he went to work on her pants, nearly toppling them onto the bed in his haste to get her naked. She laughed, and he was surprised to find himself joining in. As intense as shit was between them, this light moment almost meant more to him than the rest of it.

Then she was naked and in his arms and he stopped worrying about anything but getting her to scream his name.

Chapter Thirteen

Luke guided Alexis onto the bed. She couldn't stop another giggle from slipping free when they bounced on the mattress. Another new experience. She was racking up plenty of them when it came to him. In all the time she'd been intimate with Eric, it couldn't compare with the sheer desire she felt when Luke touched her.

And now there was an element of fun that she hadn't expected.

He kissed her, his weight settling between her legs as his tongue twined with hers. Considering how desperate he'd sounded when she was on her knees in front of him, he seemed totally content to take his time now, exploring her mouth as if memorizing the contours of it. She ran her hands up his back, trying to arch against him, but there wasn't enough leverage to get him where she needed him.

She broke away long enough to gasp. "Please, Luke."

"Please what?" He dragged his teeth down her neck as

he hooked one knee, pushing it up and out so his hard length rubbed right down her center. Another inch lower, and he'd be notched at her entrance, but he didn't push that far. Instead, he sealed their bodies again, stroking the underside of his cock against her clit, the delicious friction making her moan.

It wasn't enough. "More."

His tongue swiped down the sensitive spot where her shoulder met her neck. "Tell me what you need." The rough edge of his voice made her shiver the same way his calloused fingers did as he skated them down her thigh to cup her ass. "*Who* you need."

She laced her fingers in his hair and pulled him back into a kiss, but he didn't give her the opportunity to sink into it. He pulled back, keeping his mouth just out of reach, his body pinning her so she couldn't quite make that contact she needed. "Please."

"Tell me who makes you feel like this." He nipped her bottom lip, retreating before she was satisfied. "The only one who makes you feel like this."

There was only one right answer, and the terrifying part was it *wasn't* a lie. She'd never felt anything that could hold a candle to what Luke did to her. She loved every second of it, the way he met her challenges and took it to the next level. This wasn't a man who feared a strong woman. A broken woman.

And… She was finally starting to feel more strong than broken for the first time in her life.

Luke's fingers dug into her ass, just this side of painful. "*Who?*"

"You." She sobbed the word out, rolling her hips even

though she knew it was useless. He wouldn't be inside her until he was damn well good and ready. The waiting only made her want him more. When he didn't move, apparently willing to wait her out, she hissed out another breath. "You, Luke. You're the only one who makes me feel like this."

"Don't you dare forget it, darlin'."

Now, finally, he took her mouth again as he shifted, reaching over the bed for their packs. Anticipation curled through her, heightening the desire sparking in every place they touched. The rough skin of his scar scraped against her thigh as she hooked her free leg around his waist, that little movement sliding him against her clit and nearly enough to send her over the edge.

He knew what she was doing, the ass. Luke chuckled against her mouth. "Not yet." He pulled away enough to reach between them to roll on the condom, and then he was back, pressing against her entrance.

She expected him to shove home, the way he'd done up to this point. She *needed* him to do that.

But he worked his way into her in short, controlled thrusts, until she whimpered and strained against his hold, needing him deeper, needing him to push her over the edge of the pressure already building beneath her skin. Nothing she did helped, though.

When he was finally sheathed completely inside her, he went still. "Christ, you feel good."

"More." She clutched his shoulders, moaning when he propped himself on his elbows and shifted inside her. It wasn't enough. "I need you, Luke. Deep, hard. Make me come."

His grin was just this side of savage. "You need me."

She was too far gone to deal with the conflicting

emotions flickering over his face. All that mattered was getting him to move. "I need you." The words resonated, but she did her best to ignore it. The truth, however complicated, didn't matter right now. She'd deal with the consequences later, when she had a moment alone.

"I got just what you need." He thrust into her hard enough to make the bed frame rattle.

She reached over her head and gripped the thin metal bars, giving herself to him completely. The look on his face was reward enough, but she wasn't prepared for him to loop an arm under her waist and roll them, leaving her straddling him. Shock froze her for half a second, but his hands on her hips urged her to move.

Then pleasure took over.

"Take control. Ride me, darlin'. I want to watch your face as you come on my cock."

His words drove her on as much as his hands. She grabbed the top of the headboard and lifted herself nearly off him before slamming back down. They both moaned when she did it again. He let go of her hips to cup her breasts, lifting and squeezing, the pressure spiking her desire.

"That's right. Just like that. You're almost there."

She was. Each stroke of him inside her pushed her closer to the edge. Alexis started to close her eyes, but forced them open. She wanted to see him as pleasure took over. Needed to. It made no sense, but she was too far gone to question it.

Grinding against him, the wave of her orgasm rose and pulled her under. It kept cresting, driven by Luke's urging. He drew out her pleasure until she couldn't keep her eyes open, until her entire being was consumed with him. She was distantly aware of him finishing beneath her, but it was all she could do not to collapse on him. Her arms shook with the effort to keep herself up.

"Come here." He pulled her to his chest and cradled her there. She let herself relax into him, promising it'd only be for a little while. Then she'd get up, take a shower and…do something.

But she could enjoy this while it lasted.

Luke stroked her hair, struggling to deal with the feeling in his chest. It was soft and gooey and completely focused on the woman in his arms. She'd looked magnificent with her back arched, her hair a mess around her face, her hazel eyes hooded with pleasure, as she rode his cock. He'd never forget that image as long as he lived. He didn't want to.

Which was a goddamn problem.

He put it out of his head as he tangled his fingers in her hair and brought her up for another kiss. "Wow."

"I think that's my line." She gave him a long look, and he found himself holding his breath as she seemed to consider something. He didn't relax until she settled back down and laid her head on his shoulder again. "You can borrow it, though, because that was wow."

Another problem. Instead of scratching an itch, every time he was with her only got better. It was as if, by letting him between her thighs, she was working her way into *him.*

Guided by an urge he didn't want to ignore, he kissed the top of her head. This wasn't so bad. Right now, he didn't have to focus on how even the sex was complicated when it came to Alexis, let alone the rest of the tangled mess of emotions in his chest. He liked her. He admired her. He didn't want to see the end of his time with her.

In short, he was well and truly fucked.

"Are you going to continue being a mechanic?"

The question hit him in the stomach. He almost laid her on the bed and made some excuse—any excuse—to walk out of the room, but something stopped him. She wasn't accusing him of anything. There was only an innocent curiosity in her voice. As if she thought this was a safe subject.

Hell, it *should* be a safe subject.

He braced himself for the guilt that came with the answer. "I don't know."

Alexis lifted her head. "What do you mean?"

It was harder to put into words than he would have guessed. "It took a long time to put me back together. Even when the doc gave me the thumbs-up, I still wasn't cleared for duty. I can't meet the physical requirements anymore." And he never would again. The failure stuck in his throat. "I know that. But a part of me has been hanging on to that hope. I haven't been the best employee to my cousin, because I've been living with one foot out the door."

There was no judgment in her eyes. "Sometimes it takes a while to find your feet after the universe knocks you on your ass."

"Yeah, but it's been almost a year. It's time to get over my shit and move on—actually move on. I guess I've just been holding on to my anger, instead of looking for something productive to do with my life." He actually enjoyed working in the shop. There was something satisfying about taking a vehicle that was on its last legs and making it purr. He'd just been fighting that satisfaction every step of the way. "My auntie threatened to wallop me if I didn't pull my head out of my ass in the next few weeks."

He felt her smile against his chest. "I like this aunt of yours."

"She'd like you, too." He already knew what Aunt Rose would say about Alexis—and that she'd have hit him upside the back of the head with her purse a few times for being such an asshole initially. She would approve of Alexis's spunk and her ability to drive him up the wall. And Aunt Rose would have respected the hell out of her because she was a survivor. He didn't have to know the details to know that.

"You'll figure it out." Her quiet assurance wasn't false comfort. She actually believed that he'd be okay.

And in the face of her belief, he started to believe it for the first time, too.

Chapter Fourteen

Alexis's good mood lasted through breakfast, but took a nosedive when she caught sight of the garish tour bus. It had a picture of Maria and the von Trapp kids painted on the side and was big enough to fit fifty people. As she looked around, there were certainly enough people here to more than fill it. Her parents had done this on what her mother had called their second honeymoon. If she got on that bus, she'd be following in their footsteps.

Except she had beaten the cancer that killed her mother.

Not for the first time, she wondered if maybe their situations should have been reversed. If Mom lived, *Yé-yé* and *Nâinai* never would have moved in with Dad and taken over her and Avery's lives. Avery might be happy now, but she wouldn't have had to jump through such crazy hoops in her quest for a child. Maybe she and Drew would have seen the light earlier and saved each other a lot of pain. Her little sister would have someone to talk to about relationships and romance and everything under the sun. Their house would have been a home like it used to be.

And Alexis… She would have faded away. She wouldn't be a constant disappointment to everyone around her.

Even as the thought crossed her mind—the same way it had more times than she could begin to count—it didn't feel right. It was almost as if she was giving lip service to something she no longer felt. *I'm worth more than this. I deserve better.*

Her mother was a saint as far as she was concerned, and nothing would ever change that. But for the first time, she tried to put herself in Mom's shoes. Would she have rather lived if one of her daughters died?

No. Hell no.

Alexis stood there under the warm sun and tried to wrap her mind around the new shape of the world. If she were in her mother's place, with two daughters of her own, she'd take a bullet for either of them. What was a little cancer in the face of that? The universe didn't work like that—one life for another—but she wouldn't have hesitated to bargain with any higher power who'd listen for the lives of her daughters.

She couldn't believe her mother would feel any differently.

Mom wouldn't want me to live with regret. She'd just want me to live, to be happy, to move on.

It wasn't an easy path, but she was on it. Alexis crossed her arms over her chest, suddenly cold. *I can do this. It hasn't been easy and it's not going to get any more so, but I can do it.* She refused to fail.

She caught sight of Luke and—surprise, surprise—he was scowling. "Whatever you're thinking about, cut that shit out."

His attitude grounded her, the same way it had at the top of Pulpit Rock. She put on a brave face, though it felt a little fragile around the edges. "I know this might come as a shock to you, but you can't just glower your way in and demand that people's thoughts stop offending you."

"The world would be a better place if I could." His green eyes were filled with concern. "We don't have to do this."

He was so much easier to deal with when he was snapping at her, even if it was a surface-level attitude, and he was offering her a way out. She hadn't anticipated how raw she'd feel just staring at the bus. What was the tour itself going to do to her?

Desperate for a distraction, she blurted out, "Are your parents alive?"

"Yes."

Just that. Nothing else. "But you never talk about them."

"There's nothing to say." He shrugged. "I never knew my dad, and my mom was more concerned with her freedom than the well-being of her only child. She bounced when I was seven, and I haven't seen her since."

"Oh God. I'm sorry."

"I'm not." He hesitated, then seemed to resolve something. "I didn't go without. My Aunt Rose raised me, and I had a pretty decent childhood. What more can a kid ask for?"

Two living, loving parents. But he was right, in a way. At least he'd had family to step in and take care of him. "Tell me about your aunt. You mentioned her last night, but didn't really go into detail."

She needed this distraction. People had started filing onto the bus, and the closer they got to the door, the harder her heart pounded.

For a second, she thought he might turn her down flat. Luke had never had a problem doing that before now, but he sighed. "She's a nice lady who looks as sweet as the apple pie she bakes, but she ran a tight ship. Still does. She never hesitated to take me to task for tracking in dirt or screwing around in school." A soft smile curved his lips, and it changed the look of his entire face. He'd been attractive before, but with the obvious love there, he was absolutely stunning. "I was a little hell-raiser, but she was really good at letting me run amok and being there to help me set things right. She was the one to offer the military as an option when I didn't know what I wanted to do with my life, and she was the one to pick me up and start to put me back together when they sent me back broken."

What would her life have ended up like if her family was more like that? *Nâinai* loved the family in her own way, but she bowed to *Yé-yé's* will in all things, and Alexis's grandfather could barely stand the sight of her these days. She'd failed the family in every way that he thought counted.

Dad had done his best, and he loved her and Avery beyond a shadow of a doubt. He'd been by her side, the same as her sister, every step of the process, even though it'd torn him up in ways she could only imagine to see his daughter go through the same thing that had killed his wife. It meant that sometimes he needed to check out for a few days, and she'd always respected that, because she knew what it was like to have the past rise up and kick her in the teeth.

I did *have support and love. What happened that I let my grandparents' and ex's negativity block that out?*

She cleared her throat. "Your aunt sounds amazing."

"She is. One of a kind." He urged her toward the bus with a hand on the small of her back. "You haven't lived until you've had her pie and sweet tea."

She wasn't sure what to say to that. It wasn't likely that she'd ever meet the woman. Hell, she wasn't even sure how long Luke would stick around. Yes, he'd accompanied her to Austria, and the sex was even more outstanding now than it'd been in Ireland *and* Norway—and who would've thought *that* was possible?—but that didn't mean much in the long run.

Liar, liar, pants on fire.

He spoke as they boarded the bus and made their way to a pair of seats halfway back. "Tell me about your family."

It was the last thing she wanted to talk about—especially with the confusion of thoughts currently circling her head—but it wasn't like she could shoot him down after he opened up to her. "I have a little sister. She's bold and amazing and doesn't care what anyone thinks of her." Avery was the best part of Wellingford, even if the sight of her growing belly made Alexis hurt so much she'd taken off. The rest of her family? "Dad loves me, loves both of us." And she suddenly felt like she owed him an apology for shutting him out. "He's a good dad. The best dad. He held things together after my mom died. My grandparents moved from China and in with us not too long after that and they're...something else."

"I take it that's not a good thing."

Why did he have to choose *now* to be insightful? The bus lurched into motion and she talked faster, wishing she could outrun the demons inside her as easily as she could form them into words. "*Nâinai* isn't so bad. She's not very maternal, but she loves us as much as she can. And she makes the best cookies you'll ever try. *Yé-yé* …" Her throat felt like it was closing as the last conversation she had with him ran through her head. *We expect you at dinner, Alexis. It's the least you can do to after the mess you made of things with Eric.* Because getting cancer and being dumped by her fiancé was obviously *her* fault. "It's complicated."

"Family always seems to be."

Luke wasn't sure what he was supposed to do about Alexis. With each stop on the tour, she became more and more withdrawn, until she barely responded to anything he said. He knew what she was dreading—the gazebo—but he didn't know how to help.

The fact that he even *wanted* to help baffled him.

But this woman who didn't flinch in the face of his scars was stronger than he'd given her credit for. And now she was so obviously in pain, he wanted to wipe it away.

As they exited the bus for the third time, he followed her across the grass to the gazebo. People took turns posing for pictures, but Alexis just looked at it, her face completely still. He couldn't help thinking of the faded photograph she'd carted across half of Europe. Her parents looked so goddamn happy and in love. While he could understand the need to reclaim that, he didn't get why it was tearing her up so badly. Remembering the good times shouldn't hurt.

He searched for something to say, something to break the silence that had grown between them. "Do you want a picture?" She turned to face him and his heart stuttered to a stop when he saw the tear tracks on her face. "Alexis…"

"It's okay." Another tear fell. "You don't have to say anything. I…I just need a minute."

Did she honestly expect him to stand here and let her cry? To do nothing? Apparently she did, because she turned back to the gazebo, leaving him staring at her back. If he were smart, he'd just wait by the bus and let her ride out the storm. He didn't know how to fix this, and so he was just as likely to make it worse as he was to make it better.

But Christ, he wasn't capable of walking away.

Luke closed the distance between them and wrapped his arms around her from the back. A shudder racked her body, but she didn't shrug him off. *Thank God.*

"I'm fine."

"You don't have to be." He squeezed her, wishing he were better at this comforting shit. If his Aunt Rose were here, she'd know exactly what to say. But then, he'd gotten his tendency to take the tough-love path from her, and maybe that wasn't what Alexis needed right now. What was he supposed to say when she was falling apart in his arms?

He didn't know. So he went with the stark truth. "You can lean on me."

"I…" Another shudder, stronger this time.

God, she was killing him. "I've got you, darlin'."

Her sob broke his heart. "I miss her so much." She turned in his arms, and he gathered her against him, trying to put all the words he'd never get right into this. Alexis's entire body shook. "She shouldn't have died. She's gone and I've felt so alone for so long, and it's so selfish and I know it's selfish, but I wish she was here because I'm trying so damn hard and nothing I do is ever good enough."

He held her and let her bleed out poison that must have

been accumulating for a long time. Nothing he said could fix this, so he didn't even try. He just held her through the fury of her grief.

She kept talking, her voice barely above a whisper. "For the longest time, I was sure there was some mistake. The cancer should have taken me—not her. She would have known what to do with the second chance, and I've been floundering."

Cancer. Jesus Christ. He'd known there was something, but it'd never occurred to him that it could be *that*. Luke gathered her closer, wanting to deny the words coming out of her mouth, to shield her from the pain she'd so obviously been living with for far too long. "Alexis—"

"I was wrong. I realize that now. Even if there was some devil's bargain to be made to bring her back and take me in her place, she never would have wanted that. And…it's time to admit that I don't want that, either."

He'd thought her a spoiled princess when they first met, and the time they'd spent together had been slowly eroding that image. With this final confession, she blew it away until the only thing that remained was the real Alexis. Survivor. Stronger than she gave herself credit for. Too many things to put into words. Luke kissed her temple and held her, letting her cry it out.

He wasn't sure how much time passed, but the guide had nearly everyone back on the bus by the time she lifted a tearstained face off his shoulder and sniffed. "I'm so sorry."

"Darlin', you have nothing to apologize for." He smoothed his thumbs along her cheeks, catching a few more tears. "You've been holding that in for a long time."

"There was never time to… For any of it."

No time, and it was hellishly hard to face certain facts when a person's life was falling to pieces around them. Hell, they had so much in common, it wasn't even funny. They'd taken different paths to reach where they were, but both of them were on their own roads back to the land of the living. He smoothed her hair back. "How do you feel now?"

She swallowed. "Better, I think. I..." She looked away and then seemed to force herself to meet his gaze. "Thank you."

"Don't worry about it." For all his affected nonchalance, Luke couldn't help thinking that the balance had shifted between them. It had started in Norway, but they were rapidly reaching the point of no return. If he was going to be honest, they'd already flown straight past it.

He wasn't sure he could walk away from her now, even if he wanted to.

Chapter Fifteen

Alexis made it through the rest of the tour without any more embarrassing breakdowns, but she couldn't shake the feeling that something more profound than tears had happened back there by the gazebo. It had been like saying good-bye to Mom all over again, but this time, it felt…clean. There was no taint of sickness or the dawning horror of a family who had barely had a chance to say good-bye before they lost their rock. Maybe it was because she and Dad had been so happy here, or maybe it was because the family *had* survived. They kept living. Hell, some of them even flourished. Avery certainly had.

And as was becoming more and more clear, she hadn't done too terribly for herself, either. Yes, it seemed like the world was ending in the last few years, but she'd survived.

I survived.

She wasn't magically cured and moving on with her life, but it felt like a step in the right direction. More than that, something shifted between her and Luke back there. She kept catching him shooting unreadable looks in her direction—probably because she was doing her fair share of looking at *him*. Waiting for him to react to what she'd confessed.

But he didn't.

When he put forth the idea to come to Salzburg, she doubted he realized he was signing on for a complete emotional breakdown. Except he hadn't stood back at a safe distance. No, he'd been there to hold her up when she felt like her entire body was about to break apart. He'd held her through the storm and stood as her own personal bastion.

"What do you think about getting some food?"

She responded before her mind caught up with her mouth. "I'm not really hungry."

"I'll bet." He touched the small of her back in a move he'd been using most of the day, steering her toward a little café down a side street she hadn't noticed. "This isn't exactly an alley, but try to restrain yourself. I'm just feeding you, not luring you off to steal your virtue."

Against all reason, she smiled. "That's probably for the best. You already stole it once today."

His laughter warmed places she hadn't even realized were cold in the first place. Luke slipped his arm around her waist. "If you're lucky, I'll steal it again before the night is over."

His joking restored some of the norm to the whole situation—if walking down the street with a man she met less than a week ago after having a hurricane of an emotional meltdown on the *Sound of Music* bus tour was normal. She kept expecting him to ask questions or *something*, but he seemed to be just rolling with it. "If *I'm* lucky? Honey, you were the one pleading earlier."

His eyebrows rose. "You have a very selective memory. Pretty sure there was some *please Luke, oh my God, please* going on."

Heat stole across her cheeks, but she couldn't stifle her grin. *God, I really, really like this guy.* "Fine. We'll call this one a draw."

"Deal." He held open the door for her. "Now, food. You might not feel like it, but you need to eat."

She wasn't sure what to do with this caring side of him. "You're very mother-hen right now." She couldn't remember the last person she'd let take care of her. Avery bullied her way into it sometimes, but it had become rarer and rarer over the last few years. Alexis always said she didn't need it—she was more than capable of taking care of herself—but it was kind of nice with Luke.

He surveyed the café and then guided her to an empty table in the corner. "Goes with the territory."

"What territory is that?"

He opened his mouth, choked off whatever he'd been about to say, and gave her a strained smile. "Marines, you know."

She got the strangest feeling that he'd just lied to her. But that didn't make sense. He'd already told her he was a Marine, and the injury to his side was consistent with an IED explosion. So why the tingling on the back of her neck? She shook her head. It must be leftover tension from earlier. That was all. "I thought your lot was more point-and-shoot than caregiver."

"Yeah. A lot easier to kill than to save a life."

It was something she'd heard Ryan say more times than

she could count. Alexis frowned. "You don't know a friend of mine—Ryan Flannery—do you?" She held her breath while she waited for his answer.

Luke rolled his eyes. "What is it with you and these Flannery guys? Ex-boyfriends?"

Picturing either of the Flannery brothers as boyfriend material made her cringe, especially since Drew was currently engaged to her little sister. "Ew, no. Family friends. Ryan is a pararescuer."

He picked up the menu and scanned it. "Ah, that explains it. Those PJs are fucking crazy."

"It's been said before." And still she couldn't shake the feeling she was missing something. "Luke—"

"When were you diagnosed with cancer?"

All her breath left her in a rush. She'd known this was coming, but for him to ask her so nonchalantly blew her mind. "We're not talking about me." There was no reason to talk about it. She didn't owe him anything…except he'd been there for her when she needed him. Didn't that earn him the truth? He wasn't Eric. He was so far from Eric, it was amazing that they both occupied the same planet.

"Sure we are." He set his menu aside and propped his chin on his fists. "We've talked about me. Hell, I've told you things I haven't told anyone else. While I'm not saying that it's tit for tat, it'd be nice if you trusted me enough to return the favor."

He was right. She *knew* he was right. But it was still so hard to talk about that time. The ironic thing was that it wasn't the cancer that she was most ashamed of. It was that it had cost her both her pending marriage and her grandparents' approval. "It's hard to talk about."

"I can only imagine." The waitress approached, and he rattled off an order for each of them and then turned back to her without missing a beat. "I'm just trying to understand you. Let me in, darlin'."

This was the moment when she could open up to him, or she could shut the whole thing down. It wouldn't take much. One well-placed verbal jab and they'd be back on familiar territory and her heart would be safe. Because opening up to Luke was playing hell on her emotional state. She wished she could blame it on everything else going on, but it wouldn't be the truth.

The truth was that something settled in her chest when she was in his arms, and she craved it with a violence that was usually reserved for chocolate and *Dirty Dancing*. If she let him in now, there would be no going back.

Alexis met his sea-green eyes, and the empathy there undid her. How could she stand against a Luke who protected her?

The answer—she couldn't.

She bit her lip, seeming to waffle, and Luke held perfectly still while he waited. He could be patient when the situation called for it, and he couldn't put into words how much he wanted to know the full story. Cancer was brutal to even the strongest person, and Alexis was certainly that, but it felt like there was more to the story. Something had put its poison into her heart and twisted, and he needed to know what it was.

As the waitress set two beers in front of them, she gave

a defeated sigh. "Do you want the CliffsNotes version or the whole ugly tale?"

This would change everything between them. He was already on the fence about backing off when she went back to the States. If she gave him half a reason, he'd do everything in his power to convince her to give him a chance.

A chance at what?

Luke gritted his teeth. There was no point in fighting the truth—he'd already made a decision when it came to Alexis Yeung. He wasn't letting her get away without a fight, which meant he needed all the information he could get his hands on, no matter how uncomfortable it made him. "Tell me all of it."

Her smile wavered a bit around the edges. "I was afraid you'd say that." She took a sip of her beer. "I'm not asking for pity, okay? I'm just telling you what you asked to know."

Dread wormed its way into his gut. What the hell did she have to say that she felt the need to preface it with *that* warning? *It doesn't matter. I need to know the full story.* "Look at me, darlin'. Mine is not the face of pity."

She laughed like he'd wanted her to. "Fair point. Okay, here goes." Another drink of beer, though this time she was obviously stalling. "When my mom died, there were a lot of changes. Obviously. Like I mentioned before, my grandparents transplanted from China and came to live with us and to make sure we were brought up right." Her face twisted. "Their version of right, which included yanking me out of dance class because it didn't meet the requirements of their standard of a good Chinese woman."

He decided right then and there that someday he'd take Alexis dancing. He might not be able to keep up, but she obviously missed it. The longing was written all over her face. "They sound better and better, the more I hear."

"You aren't the only one to feel that way, but they're family." She shrugged. "The thing is, they're extremely traditional. From the time I was eighteen, they had it drilled into my head that the only way to bring honor to the family was to marry a pure Chinese man and pop out a baby or two."

The thought of her marrying someone, let alone having children with him, made him want to break something. The sheer violence of his response shocked him. Yeah, he hadn't been thrilled with her threats to chase down any man who would have her, but those were just empty promises. Marriage… That was different. Permanent. He was so busy fighting his reaction to her story, he almost missed the next part.

"So after I finished college, I ended up engaged to Eric."

Shock reared up and kicked him right in the chest. "You're *engaged*?"

"Not anymore. He broke the engagement a little over a year ago." She stared into her beer. "You see, when I was twenty-eight, I was diagnosed with cervical cancer—the same cancer that killed my mom. It wasn't as far gone as hers—not by a long shot—but I still went through a full hysterectomy and a round of chemo."

The sadness on her face hit him right where it hurt, and it was everything he could do not to reach for her. "Aw, darlin'—"

She talked right over him, as if she had to get this out or she wouldn't finish. "I'm fine. They keep an eye on it, but it hasn't come back. It might never come back." She set her beer aside. "But after the chemo was done, Eric sat me down and told me that he'd never signed on for this kind of commitment, especially when the possibility of biological children was gone." Her smile was so brittle, it felt like it actually cut him. "Besides, I was never that good in bed to begin with."

"I'll kill him." Luke twisted the cloth napkin between his hands, imagining it was that piece of shit's neck. He knew he was mangling it, but if he didn't keep himself busy, he might lose his shit right here and now.

He looked up to find Alexis's eyes unnaturally wide. "Uh… That's not necessary."

This was what she was running from. Her asshole ex who'd kicked her when she was down. What kind of man said something like that to a woman he was supposed to love enough to marry? Even more than that, what kind of man tossed a woman like Alexis to the side solely because she couldn't have biological children? She'd just survived fucking *cancer* and that's all that idiot could focus on? He gritted his teeth. "It has nothing to do with necessary. It'll be my pleasure."

"That's, uh, sweet, but no thanks." Her hand shook a little when she drank her beer. "Besides, it's nothing worse than what *Yé-yé* said afterward. I'm one gigantic black spot on the family honor, apparently."

Jesus Christ. He was half a step away from burning her whole fucking town to the ground. "Your dad sat back and let these assholes talk to you like that?"

"It's not like that." Her eyes flashed at his attack of her father. "Dad loves me regardless of if I'm following *Yé-yé's* wishes or not. And I don't think he liked Eric all that much to begin with. Avery definitely didn't."

Yeah, from what he knew of his brief interaction with

Avery last year, she would have been raring and ready to hamstring Alexis's ex after knowing he said that to her. So why didn't she? Neither Avery nor Flannery's little brother were known for their restraint. Unless… "You didn't tell your sister, did you?"

"She knows how our grandfather feels about me."

Which was a neat side step. Luke narrowed his eyes. "Do your sister and dad know about what your ex said to you?"

"They're not stupid, and Eric's timing wasn't subtle."

Which wasn't the same thing as her telling them the truth. He had a feeling that Alexis had made a habit of stuffing down her issues from the time her mother died. So her hurt and betrayal at both her grandfather and fiancé—two people who should have been at her back no matter what life threw at her—had been bottled up until she couldn't deal with it anymore, and…

Realization hit. Avery was pregnant.

That had to be the catalyst for her booking a ticket to Europe without a word of warning. Not that he could voice his realization to Alexis, because how the hell would he know that her sister was knocked up? So he set aside the knowledge and reached across the table to take her hand. "I'm going to tell you something, and I need you to perk up those pretty ears because I'm only going to say it once. You listening?"

"Not every part of me is pretty." When he just stared, she sighed. "Yes, I'm listening."

"You are a beautiful fucking person, Alexis, and your ability to have kids has absolutely nothing to do with your worth. *Nothing*. You hear me?" It wasn't like his words would magically take away the wounds of the past, but she needed to hear them spoken aloud.

And he needed to say them.

Her lower lip trembled a little, but she managed a smile and a nod. "I hear you, Luke."

Chapter Sixteen

As they walked out of the café, Alexis didn't think she'd ever felt so raw before. She'd given him everything, and he hadn't so much as balked or made a snide comment. Instead he'd looked into her eyes and voiced the one thing she'd needed to hear above all others. She wasn't sure what she was supposed to do now. Hold his hand? Kiss him? Drag him off to the nearest hostel and get him naked as quickly as physically possible? She looked around, taking in the architecture that was so prominent in the city. It was so familiar, even if she'd never walked down this street before, and it all reminded her of Mom. "I…" She cut herself off. Even now, it was so hard to put herself out there.

"Yeah?"

What the hell was the point if she didn't take a leap of faith? Or another one in the line of what felt like countless ones. "I don't want to stay here tonight." She could keep going, tell him that even the cathartic sobbing at the gazebo hadn't been enough to banish the ache of missing her mom. "Being here makes it hard to do anything but dwell in the memories, both good and bad. I just…I'm not up to it right now."

She braced herself for a glare or angry comment, but Luke only gave a short nod. "Let's see what our options are." That was it. He even took her hand as they made their way down to a corner with several cabs. He glanced at his watch. "It's getting kind of late for a flight going out, but we can see if there are any night trains."

"I've never been on a train." And she could barely reconcile this man with the one she'd met back in Cork. It was more than his taking care of her—there was something relaxed in his face that hadn't been there before. As if maybe he'd let go of some of the baggage weighing him down. She understood. It had hurt to lay the innermost part of herself out there, but she felt like she'd lanced an old wound. It would take time, but maybe she'd heal cleanly now.

Maybe his talking about his injury and potential future had done the same for him.

"Then here's to new experiences." He opened the cab door for her and followed her into the backseat. "Train station."

The cab driver muttered a confirmation and the car lurched into motion, throwing her against him. He put his arm around her shoulders. "So where else is on your list?"

She was so distracted by the insane way the cabbie was tearing through the streets, it took her a few seconds to realize he'd asked her a question. "What?"

"Your path to enlightenment or whatever you're calling it. Where else is on your list?"

This was so much easier to talk about that the relief made her feel wobbly. "There were a couple places I wanted to see just because I'm over here—Rome, Paris, Barcelona—but there's only one place left on my list. Verona."

He was silent for a few seconds. "Because…"

Right. She'd told him the reasons behind the other places. Alexis looked out the window, knowing that he could see her blush. "Juliet's Wall is there. I know the whole *Romeo and Juliet* thing is more tragedy than romance, but the wall itself has become something more. People write the name of the ones they love, and legend has it that doing so makes the love stronger." Her face was so hot, it was a wonder she didn't set fire to her skin. "And I'm sure you've heard of the letters people write to their lost loves."

"There was a movie a few years back." When she shot him a look, he shrugged. "I didn't see it, but Aunt Rose is a huge chick flick fan."

"Oh."

Luke sat back, his eyes intense despite his relaxed posture. "So you're going to go write a letter to that piece of shit ex of yours."

"What?" She burst out laughing. "God, no. Maybe I wasn't clear before, but that wasn't exactly an epic love worth writing home about." Which is why she shouldn't have been surprised by Eric's reaction to her barrenness. They'd never shared half the connection she felt with Luke.

Dangerous territory, Alexis.

She looked back out the window, trying to ignore the tension in the cab and how the scenery was flying by at a truly terrifying rate. "No, it's nothing like that. I might not have been head over heels in love with Eric, but how things fell out between us… It made me bitter. I want to let that go, and I want to open myself up to loving again."

Though she was starting to think that she didn't need a trip to Italy to accomplish that.

"Well, let's see what the train station has to offer, and then we'll see about getting you to Verona." There was a warmth in his voice that she was rapidly becoming used to. She liked grouchy Luke despite herself. A Luke who was protective and empathetic?

She more than liked him.

Alexis shut that thought down *real* fast. "Sounds great."

He pulled her back against him and tucked her against his side, his expression becoming what could only be described as mischievous. "And if you're in the mood for more new experiences, I have something in mind."

"Oh yeah?" She let herself relax against him, letting the feel of him uncoil the stress that had every muscle in her body strung tight. It felt so damn good to not have to be the strong one for once, better than she could have imagined.

He leaned down until his lips brushed her ear. She tensed, waiting for the inevitable outpouring of filthy suggestions that would get her so hot, he'd be lucky if she didn't drag him into a bathroom at the train station. But he surprised her. "You'll have to wait and see, darlin'."

"I'm not really one for surprises." Very few in her life had been good ones up to this point.

"That's a crying shame, because you're going to get one soon." He squeezed her thigh, the heat of his hand soaking through her jeans and right to her center. The bastard knew it, too, because he grinned as he sat back. "A little waiting never killed anyone." He was being downright *playful*.

"It might kill *you*." She tried to fight a grin and failed.

He laughed, the sound surprising her just as much now as it did every time it came out of his mouth. It was so at odds with the personality he presented the rest of the world, so full of joy. It made her wonder yet again what kind of man he'd been before the injury to his knee. Had he been happy? Or just another variation of the grouch she first met? The puzzle pulled at Alexis, demanding she ask him the same probing questions he'd subjected her to.

But then she looked at his face, the grin that made her want to smile right back, the mischief lighting up his green eyes, and realized it didn't matter. She wasn't the same person she'd been before the cancer, and for the first time, she was really okay with that. She was stronger now, more in charge of her own life. It didn't matter what Luke was before his injury, because it was part of the journey that had made him into the man he was today. That was all that mattered.

The cab screeched to a halt in front of the train station, and Luke paid before she had a chance to go for her wallet. "You don't have to do that. I'm not exactly short on money." One of the benefits of working as a nurse and basically being a shut-in the rest of the time was that her savings account wasn't hurting in the least.

"It has nothing to do with what I have to do and everything to do with what I want to do." He climbed out and held the door open for her. "You're so damn strong, darlin'. Let me take care of you in this one little way."

He kept staying that. She knew she was stronger than she used to be, but stronger didn't mean *strong*. She hadn't felt very strong a few hours ago when she was sobbing her heart out, but she wasn't about to argue with him. "Just don't get used to it."

"I wouldn't dream of it."

The train station was nearly deserted, but there were small groups here and there who seemed either to be waiting for a train or to have just gotten off one. She spotted a bathroom and touched his arm. "I'm going to change into something more comfortable." If they were taking a night train, her jeans weren't the best option for lounging.

And frankly, she wanted to give Luke as easy access as she could for whatever he had planned. If she managed to drive him a little crazy in the process… Well, she was okay with that, too.

Luke scanned the destinations. There were two trains leaving in the next hour, one to Frankfurt and one to Venice. Easy choice. He bought the tickets, paying extra to make sure they were in a sleeper car by themselves. He had a promise to keep, after all. When he turned around, he stumbled to a stop at the sight of Alexis. She'd changed in the bathroom, and now wore a long dress that was made of some bright print that defied explanation. As she drew closer, she raised her eyebrows and held her jacket apart, and he realized two things simultaneously.

With the light coming in behind her, the damn thing was nearly sheer.

And she wasn't wearing a fucking thing underneath it.

He glanced around, but no one seemed to be paying them a bit of attention. Thank God, because he wasn't about to get arrested for murdering some idiot who caught an eyeful of her. He stalked over. "You're going to pay for that little stunt, darlin'."

"It's worth it." She eyed the tickets in his hand. "Where are we going?"

"Surprise." He said it mostly to push at her, to make her pay for the way she made him feel knowing there was only a thin layer of cloth between her skin and the rest of the world. It didn't matter that her jacket covered her from the tops of her thighs to her neck. All he cared was that she'd intentionally teased him.

Two could play that game.

Alexis trailed after him as he made his way to the train marked on the tickets. "Have I mentioned how little I like surprises?"

"At least once." He handed the man in uniform the tickets and motioned for her to precede him through the door. "After you."

She didn't look particularly happy with him, but that was okay. They had plenty of time for him to get her back in the right state of mind. And Luke knew exactly how to start.

As they made their way deeper into the car, he picked up his pace until he was damn near pressed against her back. "I like that dress."

"Hmm? This old thing?"

"I like it so much, I'm going to rip the damn thing off with my teeth later. But not before I push it up your thighs and stroke that sweet pussy of yours until you're begging for me."

She stumbled, and he used it as an excuse to steady her—and pull her back to press his cock against her ass. Her gasp was audible even over the hum of the engine.

Alexis shook him off, but it took her a few seconds to move forward. Her voice didn't sound steady as she shot over her shoulder, "We'll see."

"Playing hard to get? I'm hurt."

"I doubt it." She glanced back, a wicked grin on her face. "Where are our seats?"

"This way." He slid past her, using entirely more contact than strictly necessary. "Follow me."

"Better than walking around with you staring at my ass."

He laughed. "It's an amazing ass."

"I know."

As promised, they had a sleeper car to themselves. The room was minuscule, with a twin bed on each side and just enough room between them for a person to stand.

It was perfect.

"Why, Luke, if I didn't know better, I'd say you lured me back here to take advantage of me." She dropped her bag on the bed on the left side and sat down next to it.

He sank onto the mattress next to her, intentionally crowding her, but didn't say anything as he arranged his bag next to hers. After a little while, the train rumbled into motion. No one else had walked past them, which suited him just fine. Still, he sat back and waited.

It didn't take long for the attendant to come through, double-check their tickets, and disappear again. Good. They shouldn't have any interruptions from this point on. He slid the door closed and then locked it. When he turned and glanced at Alexis, he nearly laughed at the furious way her toe tapped. Poking at her was downright enjoyable.

As expected, she lasted less than five minutes after the train left the station behind. "You mentioned a surprise."

Gotcha. "I thought you weren't sure which way you were landing on the subject."

She crossed her arms under her breasts. "Don't make me take off the jacket."

"As a threat, that's sorely lacking." He curled a strand of her dark hair around his fingers. "Take off the jacket."

She grinned. "Maybe I'm cold."

"Now you're just being contrary. I'll keep you warm, darlin'. Cross my heart." He used a single finger to trace an *X* over his heart. The motion felt strangely intimate, as if he were promising more than sex. Hell, he kind of was. He'd already come to terms with the fact that he didn't want this thing with her to end when she left Europe.

He just needed to convince her to give him a shot.

"How can I say no to a promise like that?"

"Simple. You can't." He used his free hand to drag the hem of her dress up to her knees. "Your skin is so soft. It's practically begging for my mouth."

Her lips parted. "Too much longer, and my skin isn't going to be the only thing that's begging."

"That so?" Luke kept moving the fabric up, until it hit the tops of her thighs. He nudged her legs apart. "Darlin', I haven't even gotten started."

She made a sound fantastically close to a whimper. "That's what I was afraid of."

"It's a long train ride, after all. Wouldn't want to wear you out too soon." He traced an abstract pattern on the inside of her thigh closest to him, moving up with agonizing slowness. "That wouldn't be very gentlemanlike."

"I hate to be the one to tell you this, Luke." She hissed out a breath as his thumb feathered over the dip where thigh met hip. "But you wouldn't know a gentleman if he hit you in the face."

"Now, that's just mean." He finally gave in to the temptation to cup her. "No panties. That was mean, too. Do you know what went through my mind when you opened that jacket and gave me an eyeful of those perky nipples and that delicious vee between these thighs?"

"No." She spread her legs wider, giving him better access, her breathing coming in short gasps.

"Lose the jacket and I'll tell you."

She leaned forward and struggled to get it off. The move pressed her more firmly against his hand, and he couldn't fight back a groan when his fingers slid through her wetness. She was ready for him. If he said to hell with it and knelt between her legs, she'd spread them and take his cock deep. She wouldn't even hesitate.

But that wasn't part of the plan, no matter how much he wanted to be buried inside her right now.

Alexis tossed the jacket on top of their bags and leaned back against the seat, her hazel eyes on him. Her dress had slipped a bit, and it would only take the barest nudge to have it dipping further and revealing a nipple. He helped it along, sliding the strap off her shoulder so that her breast was bared, much the same way it'd been that day up on the cliff.

This time he wasn't going to let anything stop them.

Chapter Seventeen

We're practically in public.

The thought was on repeat as Alexis arched up to meet Luke's mouth, his hand between her legs making her feel both powerful and needy, branding her as his and setting her free, and a thousand other impossible things. It didn't matter if there was a locked door between them and the rest of the train. The feeling of being semipublic made her crazy in the best way possible. His tongue twining with hers only made the feeling more intense.

He kissed down her neck and over her chest to the breast he'd freed. When his mouth closed around her nipple, she nearly cried out. Only the fact that there might be people in the next car over kept her silent—and ramped up the desire pumping through her body.

He knew. Of course he knew. Luke lifted his head as he plunged a finger into her. "Better be quiet, darlin'. Someone might hear your whimpers and come to investigate."

That accent should be illegal, especially when it was whispering such dark and dirty things to her. She bit her lip as he hitched her right leg up, baring her completely and leaving her open to whatever the hell he wanted to do her with his hand. All the while, his gaze never left her face. "You like that."

"Don't know what you're talking about."

"Of course you don't." He spread her wetness up and over her clit, pausing to circle it once, and then again. "Like you're not about to come just thinking about someone walking in on us. Just imagine the picture they'd see." As he spoke, he used his thumb to press against her clit as he thrust his finger into her. "You, with your dress up around your hips, my hand between your legs." He used his free hand to pull down the other strap of her dress, leaving her naked from the waist up. Hell, from the waist down, too. "Anyone could see you. All of you."

"Yes."

"Yes?" He took his hand away, and she almost sobbed out a protest. "Wrong answer, darlin'." Before she could say anything, he shifted, sliding to his knees and pushing her legs up and out. "The only one who gets to see you like this is *me*. Say it."

His first slow drag of tongue over her clit nearly stole her ability to breathe, but she still managed to grind out the words. "You're the only one."

"Darlin', I'm the only one, period." Another lick. "I'm the only one who's going to lick this pretty pussy, and I'm sure as fuck the only one who gets to fuck you until you scream my name."

She fisted her hands in her dress as he continued the

slow, exploring licks. It was tempting to give herself over to how good he made her feel, but his words were on a different level than they'd been up to this point. This wasn't just possessive dirty talk. He was practically declaring his intentions to… She couldn't let it go. "What are you saying?"

He shifted, shoving two fingers into her as he sucked her clit into his mouth, setting his teeth against the sensitive flesh. Shock had her slapping her hand over her mouth to stifle her cries as his assault shoved her into a free fall. By the time she came down, he'd gentled his ministrations to the barest brushing of lips against her heated skin.

Then Luke slid back onto the bed and pulled her up to straddle his lap. She could only cling to his shoulders and shake as he undid his jeans and shoved them down his thighs. A whimper slipped free as she slid against his hard length, not up enough to let him in, but just enough to tease. God, she wanted.

He stilled her with his hands on her hips. "Condom, darlin'."

Condom. Right. She'd been dangerously close to forgetting that one little fact. Pregnancy wasn't a factor but… "Should I be worried about you?"

The shock on his face nearly made her laugh. "I haven't been with anyone in over a year. I'm clean."

She kissed him. "I can't get pregnant, Luke. I want to feel you. All of you."

"Are you sure?" He groaned when she slid against him again. "Darlin', be sure before you say shit like that."

"I'm sure." It might have only been a few days, but how did such a relatively short time hold up against the fact that they'd bared their souls to each other? Like called to like, and she and Luke were the same in too many ways to discount. He understood her like no one else in her life did, and she might be the first person to look at him and see the scars as just another part of the man. They didn't make him less. They were simply a part of his journey that other people could see.

She wanted this closeness, too—a physical closeness to match the emotional one that seemed to grow with each passing hour. She reached between them and took him in hand, guiding him to her entrance.

He pulled her down onto him, sealing them as close as two people could be. Then he hooked the back of her neck and held her far enough away to force her to meet his eyes as he used the other hand on her hip to slide her up and down his cock. "To answer your earlier question… I'm saying I want you, all of you, only you. I want you on my cock, in my bed, and in my life."

She moaned as he brought her down, grinding against her clit. "That's all?"

"Darlin', that's *everything*." He kissed her, the softest, sweetest kiss of her entire life, as if she mattered more than breathing. She clung to him, riding him as pressure tightened low in her body, pushing her closer and closer to oblivion with each thrust.

"Luke—"

"I know. I've got you."

His words—the same words he'd whispered earlier that day—unleashed the pleasure inside her. He kissed her, swallowing her scream and drawing out her orgasm, until her entire world narrowed down to the feeling of his hands on her hips, his cock filling her completely, and his mouth on hers.

He was right. This was everything.

Luke cradled Alexis against his chest and just let himself be. There was nowhere he had to go, nothing he was supposed to be doing, nothing weighing him down. For the first time since his injury, he actually felt at peace. He stroked her hair back from her face and pressed a kiss to her forehead. "I mean it."

"Hmm?"

"Every word I said. I mean it." He wasn't ready to start throwing around certain four-letter words, but it was time to stop ignoring the connection between them. For the first time in nearly two years, he felt alive and worth a damn, and it was because of the woman blinking sleepily at him.

She gave him a tentative smile. "It's okay, Luke. You get a free pass on anything said in the heat of the moment."

That was the thing, he didn't *want* a pass. "Darlin', don't think you're getting out of this that easily." He lifted her and set her back down in his lap, her legs on one side and her head against his shoulder.

"Will you…" She took a deep breath. "Will you tell me about how you hurt your knee? The full story?"

Every instinct screamed for him to change the subject or snap at her or do anything other than take that fun little trip down memory lane. But hadn't he asked her exactly that back at the café? It was only fair to trot out his wounds for her inspection.

But as he looked down at her face, he knew it wasn't curiosity driving her. She caught him watching her. "It's a huge part of your life—of who you are now. I just… I feel like you know all the ugly parts of me, and maybe it's not fair to ask for you to lay yourself bare the way I did earlier, but I'd like you to tell me. If you want to." She smiled. "I already know that you love your auntie, even if she's a tough lady, and that you're going to be okay. You might feel like you stalled out, but you've been moving in the right direction all along. And you're proud and stubborn and know how to drive a woman out of her mind with pleasure."

"Not a woman. You. Only you, darlin'."

She bit her lip as if she didn't quite believe him. "But my point is, I'd like to know more about that pivotal part of your life."

If he was serious about pursuing this thing with her, it meant he had to open up about the specifics at some point. It might as well be now. He considered how to tell the story without giving away that he'd been a PJ. At least he didn't have to edit out Flannery—he'd been sent to the northern base in Afghanistan, while Luke ended up at the southern one. "All clusterfucks start out as routine missions, and this one was no exception. We were in the area for some recon." Or at least the Marines he was accompanying were. PJs normally didn't head out on shit like that, but there'd been a report of an injured soldier in the area, and they were tasked with finding him and keeping him alive until they got to the hospital. "No one knew it was an active minefield."

"Oh, honey."

He shook his head. "Part of the job description."

"Just because you know it's a risk doesn't mean you have to bear it all with your chin up." She cuddled closer and kissed his shoulder. "Sorry. I'll keep quiet."

Having her in his arms made it easier to keep going.

"I had our patient over my shoulders. The guy next to me, Barger, took a wrong step. I didn't even have time to register what happened when I was flying through the air." The world had dissolved to pain and red and a roaring in his ears. "I don't remember much after that." The PJ still in the helicopter had filled in the details. How Barger was beyond saving, and how the blast had severed an artery in his leg, killing him within minutes. *That* was the hardest part to live with—knowing that he hadn't saved his friend. Yes, he'd saved the man they were sent in for, but it wasn't enough. "I woke up in the hospital in Landstuhl. They'd done what they could at the local base, and they saved my life, but they weren't worried about making me pretty."

He paused, half expecting her to cut in with something, some meaningless apology, or an assurance that he really was a hero even though he'd failed his teammate. He should have known better. Alexis didn't do any of that. She just pressed another kiss to his neck and hugged him tight. "I'm glad you lived."

"I am, too." If he hadn't, there would be no ridiculous mission sending him across Europe after this woman who seemed to see the man beneath the scars, this woman who was stronger than she gave herself credit for, who'd given him a gift beyond measure. "It was a long recovery, and the doc sat me down three weeks into it and flat out told me that I'd never regain full motion in my knee, and the muscle damage meant it'd always cause me problems, no matter how hard I worked."

This part, strangely enough, was harder to get out than the rest. "I went into the military straight out of high school. It gave me a purpose I was missing. It was my everything."

"You lost your identity and purpose in one fell swoop."

Exactly. "I'm not proud of it. Seems a man should be more than his job." But everything about Luke had been wrapped up in the PJs. Without that...What was left? He laid his cheek against her hair as the answer came to him for the first time that he'd been wrong—he was more than the PJs. He was a nephew and a mechanic and a man. More than that, he was a survivor.

And the woman in his arms was the one who'd forced him to realize it.

Chapter Eighteen

Alexis woke up wrapped around Luke. It was a really nice place to be. She took the opportunity to study his sleeping face. His beard was a little longer, and he looked tired even while sleeping, but some of the tension that had become so familiar was gone. It made sense. He'd been carrying around a burden to rival hers for a long time. It was enough to make her shake her head. Someone would have to search to find two people as messed up as they were. And yet…they seemed to fit each other.

Maybe all a person needed was someone to stop long enough to try to really understand where they'd come from.

Luke had done that and more—he'd given her back a part of herself she'd been searching for. And maybe, just maybe, she'd done a little of the same for him. She reached up and cupped his jaw, sliding her hand over the scruff. He opened his eyes. "You were watching me sleep."

"Guilty as charged."

He stretched beneath her and yawned. "I guess I can live with that."

The train chose that moment to slow, nearly toppling her off his lap. Luke caught her before she fell and lifted her back onto the bed. "We're almost there."

She looked out the window, her eyes widening when she caught sight of… "Canals. We're in Venice?"

"I figured Verona could wait a few days, since Venice is on the way. New experiences, remember?"

"This trip is full of them." She accepted her bag when he passed it over and slipped on her jacket. Then she followed him toward the same door they'd come in. The early-morning sun hit her face, and she couldn't help smiling. "This is amazing. I've only read about this place in one of the many travel books I've checked out over the years. Thank you, Luke."

He took her hand. "Bri must be delighted that one of the Yeung sisters actually darkens the door of the library from time to time."

The world took a slow turn, and reality slammed into her hard enough to steal her breath. She looked at him, willing the words to have not just come out of his mouth. But Luke only looked at her with an expectant expression, waiting for her reply. She took her hand from his and stumbled away. "You…"

"Darlin', what's wrong?"

Everything. She could barely hear him over the pounding in her head. All the times she'd thought his story didn't quite line up and convinced herself she was being paranoid. She'd been right all along. The only way he could know that Bri ran the library back in Wellingford was if he knew Ryan.

Luke moved to take her hand, but she backed out of reach. "Don't touch me."

"Alexis, what's wrong?"

He hadn't even realized his slip. A small, traitorous part of her wanted to keep her mouth shut and cling to what they had. But she'd be clinging to a lie, and she'd learned the hard way that the truth would use the first opportunity to rise up and punch her in the throat just like it'd done so many times before. Accusations flew to her lips, driven by an anger she clung to because the only other option was to face the all-encompassing loss threatening to take over. "Ryan asked you to come, didn't he?" It was the only option. No one else in their group had the military background and contacts to call in a favor like this.

Luke went still and then closed his eyes. "Shit."

Any hope that she'd had of being wrong disappeared as his shoulders slumped. It was true. Ryan and Drew and her sister hadn't trusted her enough to let her do this alone. That hurt almost as much as the realization that Luke had been lying to her this entire time. "How do you know him?"

He opened his eyes. "We were PJs together."

The bottom of her stomach dropped out. He wasn't even a goddamn Marine. Had anything he said over the last week actually been true? "Wow."

"I'm sorry. I didn't mean for it to get this out of control."

"That's the best you have? When were you going to tell me the truth?" She took another step back. "When I asked you to meet my family and friends? Or were you just going to smile and pretend they hadn't sent you to keep me in line? God, you're such a damn liar."

"You were going to invite me home with you?" He

shook his head as if trying to clear it. "Just hold on." He held up his hands, but didn't try to approach. "I meant what I said last night and this morning."

"What part? The part where you said you wanted more with me? Or the part where I'm worth more than a womb?" Tears clogged her throat, but she refused to let them free. It was a lie. Her independence. Her freedom. Her actually starting to feel like she might have found the missing part of herself. All of it. "Did Ryan tell you exactly what to say to make me feel like I was actually accomplishing something over here? You must have gotten a good laugh over it."

"I didn't do shit except chase after you. You did the rest yourself."

"You mean babysit. Did he tell you to sleep with me, too? It must have been difficult to get over your distaste for the spoiled little princess long enough to get me into bed. You really took one for the team." She'd thought she experienced heartbreak when Eric sat her down to tell her it was over.

It was nothing compared to this.

Luke's mouth went tight. "Enough, Alexis. We can talk this out."

She jerked back, feeling like he'd reached out and slapped her. *Stop it. Stop it right now before you say something you can't take back.* But it was too late. Hurt and betrayal welled up inside her, taking over, until she could barely look him in the face. "Ryan wasn't just babysitting *me* when he called you in. Two birds, one stone, Luke."

He flinched, some of the warmth draining out of his eyes. "You took your fate into your own hands, and you succeeded. This self-pity bullshit isn't hurting anyone but yourself."

The need to strike out, to expel some of this horrible feeling in her chest, was overwhelming. *It was all a lie.* "Don't hold back. Tell me what you really think. Though my so-called self-pity can't stand against *yours*."

His mouth tightened. "There's the spoiled little princess again, throwing a tantrum because the world isn't how she thought it should be."

God, it was a miracle she could keep breathing past the pain. "Better than sitting around, nursing old hurts. At least I tried to move on with my life. You're—you're happy being miserable." She couldn't do it anymore. If she stood here a second longer, she was going to burst into tears, and he didn't deserve to see that he affected her enough to cry. "Good-bye, Luke. I'd say it was nice knowing you, but all it did was confirm what I knew the moment I saw you. You're an arrogant asshole with a bad attitude."

"Keep walking, princess. That's what you do, isn't it? Run away when things get hard."

It's not being a coward if I have to flee to keep from throwing myself in your arms and begging you to make it all okay. But it would be a lie—the last in a long line of many. She deserved better than that. And he deserved better than to be tied with a woman he'd only followed around as a favor to a former squad mate.

Luke let her go. He stood there and watched her walk away, disappearing into the crowd on the train platform. It wasn't so easy to banish her words. He tried to dredge up some anger, annoyance, *anything* to avoid dealing with the gaping wound opening up inside him, but it wouldn't come.

Of course she couldn't wait around long enough to actually talk about this. She'd gotten some news she didn't like and taken off. Just like she always did.

He shook his head. That reasoning didn't stick anymore, not now that he knew her. She might have run from Wellingford, but she'd put up with a lot of shit before she did. And she was right—he'd been floating angrily through life since the IED went off. But he'd been about to start making changes. *She* inspired that.

Alexis had made him take a step to the side and really look at what his life could be like if he wasn't so determined to cling to what he'd lost. Being around her amazing strength was enough to have him feeling like he could conquer anything.

Like he was more than the sum of his scars.

What the hell am I supposed to do now?

Luke cursed. "Chase her down, you idiot." He might have lied to her about why he was in Europe in the first place, but he hadn't lied about anything else. Hell, he'd been more truthful and real with her than he had been with anyone else in years. He couldn't let her just walk away.

He started in the direction she'd gone, nearly shoving people out of his way. A flash of dark hair caught his eye, and he rushed over and spun the woman around. The woman who was *not* Alexis. "Shit, I'm sorry. Wrong person."

She glared and rattled off something angry in Italian before hitching her purse higher on her shoulder and stalking away. *Fuck*. He turned a full circle, but there was no sight of Alexis. Which made sense. She wasn't going to stick around and wait for him to pull his head out of his ass. Maybe it was for the best. What use did a woman like her have for him?

Yeah, he was half a step from declaring something a whole lot more permanent than infatuation, but he was still broken in a big way. Her words only showed exactly how well she understood that.

You're talking a good game because your goddamn heart is breaking, you fool.

Yeah, he was.

He should probably call Flannery and give him an update, but Luke didn't have it in him right now. In order to explain why he wasn't chasing her down, he'd have to tell the man he'd been crossing the line with Alexis from day one. That wasn't a conversation he needed right now—or ever.

No, what he needed right now was a drink, preferably a double.

As he walked down the street, he wished he could appreciate the beauty of Venice, but the warm colors, ancient buildings, and countless bridges arching over the canals had nothing on Alexis. Christ, why hadn't he gone after her immediately? The few minutes it took to shove his pride into the backseat was all she needed to run away. Yeah, she might not want to see him right now, but at least then he'd know she was safe.

He shook his head. That was a dirty lie. She was more than capable of taking care of herself. She'd proven that every step of the way. *He* was the one constantly trailing after her, bullying his way into her life in an effort to feel like he was worth a damn.

She didn't need him. She never would.

A sign hung from a building up ahead, the picture of pizza and beer a promising one. If he was going to be in Italy, he might as well try the pizza, even if eating was the last thing he felt like doing right now. Still, the drink was high on his list, so he pushed through the door.

The room was deserted, faded wood tables and chairs without a single occupant. Even the bar running along the back of the room was empty. He almost turned around and walked out, but a dark-haired woman poked her head out from a doorway he hadn't seen. She rattled something off in Italian, but the shooing motion couldn't be clearer. They obviously weren't open.

"My bad."

"Whoa, hold on. American?"

He shrugged. "Yeah. Mississippi."

"Awesome." She jerked a thumb at herself. "New York, born and raised." The woman paused as if considering him. "Look, we aren't really open, but if you want…"

"A beer." He felt like a drowning man flailing for a life preserver.

She laughed. "Dude, it's nine a.m., but whatever floats your boat. If you want a beer, you can hang out and drink while I open."

The ability to drink without worrying about some stranger trying to talk to him? If he didn't feel like his heart had been ripped out of his chest, he might actually smile. "I'd appreciate that…"

"Tristina."

"Luke."

She disappeared under the bar and came up with a bottle. "Here. You look like you could use it."

"You have no idea." The first sip didn't do a damn thing to wash away the last week. Hell, he wasn't sure an entire brewery would be enough to erase how it felt to have Alexis in his arms. He was so fucked it wasn't even funny.

"Try me."

When he raised his eyebrows, she shrugged and laughed. "Bartender is just another word for shrink. The fact that I'm bilingual only makes it worse. I have people telling me their sob stories in both English *and* Italian. But the upside is it makes me really great at solving other people's problems. And I've been doing this long enough to know that you have problems. It's written all over your face."

He almost begged off, but the truth was that he didn't have another person in this world he could talk to about Alexis. Flannery would threaten his life, and Aunt Rose might actually fly her fifty-seven-year-old ass out here just to smack him upside the back of the head with her purse. "You sure?"

"Definitely. Hit me with it." She opened a cabinet and started stacking glasses on the bar. "I guarantee I've heard it all before."

"I'm retired military. Former squad mate of mine called in a favor and asked me to keep an eye on a family friend out here who was traveling alone. Which is fine, except I fell for her in the process. Today she figured out that I'm not a stranger she met in a bar, and that I was lying to her this entire time."

Tristina's dark eyes were wide. "Okay, I lied. I've never heard that one before. You said you're falling for this girl?"

The truth was he'd passed that bridge yesterday when he held her while she cried and watched her pull herself together. Or maybe it was back on the top of Pulpit Rock when she faced down her fears to prove to herself she could. Or, hell, if he was going to be honest, the whole damn thing had started the moment she took out his bum leg in a back alley in Cork. "Head over heels."

"Then why the hell are you sitting in my bar? Go get her."

"It's not that simple." Even thinking about the look of betrayal on her face made him sick to his stomach. She was entitled to it, too. "She hates me."

"If she let you hike around Europe with her, she doesn't hate you. She's probably wicked pissed, but you totally deserve that for lying to her."

He drained half his beer. "Not really helping."

"Nah, hear me out. Pissed isn't forever—pissed is all surface-level hurt. You just have to man up and prove to her that what's between you isn't a lie. Simple." Tristina grimaced and tucked her long hair behind her ears. "Okay, maybe not exactly simple, but it's doable."

It was easier said than done. He didn't get the feeling that Alexis would stand still and talk with him. It was far more likely that she'd take out his knee and walk away while he was still trying to fight through the pain. "How the hell am I supposed to do that?"

"Hell if I know." She laughed. "I just work here. But I can tell you that sitting at this bar, drinking a beer by yourself, isn't the way to go."

Which meant he needed to find her. That, at least, he had a head start on. Luke finished his beer and pushed to his feet. "What do I owe you?"

"It's on the house." She grinned. "Can't put a price on entertainment."

He snorted. "Thanks."

"No problem. Now go get your girl."

Chapter Nineteen

Alexis walked for hours, blind to the sights around her. All she could focus on was the betrayal soaking through her body, poisoning every memory of her time with Luke. He'd lied to her from the start. He'd been playing a part perfectly designed to make her feel like she was actually accomplishing what she set out to do here. Would she have done half of it if he weren't there, prodding her along?

She didn't know, and that was going to haunt her for the rest of her life.

When she finally started to notice her surroundings, the sun was sinking into the horizon. *Shit.* She needed to find a place to stay, and quickly. Walking around a strange city at night was asking for something bad to happen. She paused and dug through her bag, coming up with the lodging book she'd been using to pick out places to stay. Flipping to Venice, she picked the first hotel that looked familiar, not having the patience to deal with a hostel and the risk of sharing her room with other people. All she wanted right now was to be alone and mourn the loss of something she'd apparently never had to begin with.

Finding the hotel took longer than she would have liked, and by the time she walked into the lobby, it was fully dark. At least the clerk made checking in relatively painless, and ten minutes later, she was finally alone. Alexis locked the door and dropped her pack on the floor.

Then she tore off her jacket and stripped out of the dress. She'd never wear the damn thing again. Hell, she should cut it into a thousand tiny pieces and flush it down the toilet. Even feeling the flimsy fabric against her skin was a reminder of Luke's hands on her body and the feeling of completion that only seemed to come with his mouth on hers and his cock sheathed deep within her. And the things he'd said to her, the beautiful things that made her feel like being whole and strong wasn't just a possibility, but inevitable. All gone. All lies.

The only thing she'd done in Europe without him was visit the Blarney Stone. Not exactly the actions of the strong and fearless woman she'd started to feel like. Without Luke by her side, she never would have made it to the edge of that cliff. After a spectacular failure like that, would she have even bothered to try her next destination? Or would just have booked a flight and gone home with her tail between her legs?

She didn't know.

Loss nearly made her double over. The lie was bad enough, but he'd taken away every single thing she'd accomplished in the process, stripping away New Alexis and leaving broken and battered Old Alexis in her place.

Moving on autopilot, she picked up the single phone in her room and went through the steps for an international call. She had no idea what time it was back home, and she didn't care. Avery was going to hear what she had to say, one way or another.

Her sister answered on the third ring. "Hello?"

All the anger and frustration that had been brewing inside her since she realized Luke had been sent by Ryan bubbled up her throat, making it hard to breathe. "How could you?"

"Alexis?"

"Who else would it be?" Her laugh tore from her throat. "Why, Avery? Do you really think I'm so goddamn helpless that I can't take care of myself? You *knew* how much I needed this!"

Her sister sighed. "He told you."

"No. He was plenty happy to go along with the lie until kingdom come. But he slipped up." She gripped the phone tighter, the storm of emotions inside her making her voice ugly. "You should pay him extra, though. He really went above and beyond the call of duty."

"God, Alexis, you took off without a word to anyone. For all I knew, you were heading to that giant-ass cliff to throw yourself off. If our positions were reversed, you would have done the same damn thing."

"*You should have trusted me.* I needed time and space to get my head on straight."

"Then you should have planned your trip like a normal person instead of running away."

Having Luke's words thrown back in her face made her knees give out. She slumped onto the bed. "So you sent a babysitter."

"It was Ryan's idea, but I supported it. I'm not going to apologize for worrying about you, so if that's what you're looking for, you're out of luck. I did what I thought was best."

"And whose idea was it to have Luke fuck me into submission and say all the right things? Because that was a cold goddamn decision."

A beat of silence passed, and then another. "I think you're going to need to repeat that."

"Which part—you all back home being assholes, or the part where Luke followed orders and blew my mind seven ways to Sunday?" A sob worked its way up her throat, escaping before she could hold it back. "I cared about him, Avery. I thought it was real."

"Hold, please."

Like she was going anywhere. All she wanted to do was crawl under the covers and cry until she didn't feel anything anymore. She pushed back to her feet, but there wasn't enough phone line to pace. "Sure. Whatever."

"Thanks." The sound was muffled, but she still heard a thump and a curse. Avery sounded so damn vicious, even Alexis winced. "Drew Flannery, I'm going to kill your brother, and I'm not even going to bother to make it look like an accident. What made Ryan think it was a good goddamn idea for Jacks to seduce my sister?"

Drew's voice was a little farther away, but still clear. "What the hell are you talking about?"

"They've been knocking boots, bumping uglies… Do we really have to go through this again?"

"*I'm going to kill that slimy little fuck.*"

A rustling, and then Avery was back. "I think it's pretty

safe to say that no one asked Jacks to bang you, and you might want to tell him that next time he's in Wellingford, the Flannery brothers are going to knock his teeth in."

The back of her legs hit the bed and she let herself fall onto it. Again. They hadn't set him out to seduce her? Not that she really believed that either Drew or Ryan would give the green light on something like that—it was too cold for them—but that didn't mean a damn thing. The thing between her and Luke wasn't real. *Nothing* had been real since their encounter in the alley. "But... What about all the stuff he said?"

"Honey, I don't have the slightest idea what you're talking about. We sent him out there to make sure you didn't jump to your death or get murdered or taken into the slave trade. That was it. He wasn't even supposed to be in contact with you if there was a choice in the matter."

His words rolled through her. *It was real, darlin'. All of it.* "I... He lied to me." He said what he needed to in order to keep her moving, keep her thinking she was doing things on her own when all along there'd been a safety net in place. A safety net she hadn't asked for or wanted.

"Yeah, that was kind of in the job description." The connection dissolved into static, and when it came back, Avery sounded calmer. "I have no idea what happened between you two, but if you want to share, I'm listening."

"So you can send someone else out here to clean up the mess?"

"Good God, Alexis, cut it out. I want you happy, and if you're going to promise me you'll be safe, then I'll do my damnedest to sit on my hands until you come home." She paused. "You...are coming back, right?"

There was no question. As stifling as Wellingford had become over the last few months, it was still home. She couldn't imagine herself anywhere else. And beyond that, she had a little niece or nephew coming into the world in a very short amount of time. She'd have to be a lot worse off to actually walk away from her family. "Yeah, I think so."

"Thank God."

Though part of her wanted to keep on the path of her righteous anger, she couldn't do it. The truth was, she missed her sister. This was the longest they'd ever gone without talking, and it was downright unnatural. So she took a shuddering breath and let go of the rage that had taken the driver's seat for most of the day. "I went to Austria and saw the gazebo."

"The one—"

"Yeah. It was just like in the picture. I…I actually felt close to her there for the first time in a long time." She took a shaky breath. "I miss her, Avery. It's like losing her all over again, but it feels cleaner this time. I'm glad I went." Glad that she'd finally faced all the fears she'd kept hidden in her heart of hearts. *That* had felt real, no matter that it was a lie that had taken her to Austria with Luke by her side.

"Did you find what you were looking for?"

That was the question, wasn't it? She thought back over the last week, over the things she'd seen and the places she'd gone. Over her fights with Luke and the nights that lit her entire body on fire. Over the way he'd bared himself to her so completely, and hadn't flinched when she'd returned the favor. *Why would he flinch? He knew everything before getting on a plane to come after me. That wasn't acceptance. That was him playing a part to make me feel like I was actually stronger than I am.* "I wish you hadn't sent him."

"Honey, whatever you think he did, I should be the first to tell you—Jacks is a really shitty actor. The man wears his thoughts on his face like nobody's business. I actually won a pretty penny from him playing poker last time he was in town visiting Ryan."

"But..." He *had* been a giant asshole when they first met. Even when he'd dragged her up to his room, he'd been angry. It was only in Norway that some of that finally started to break, and then fall away completely in Salzburg. She wanted to keep silent, but the thought circling her mind had to be voiced. "I fell for him, Avery. So hard that I don't know which way is up."

"Luke's a good guy." Her sister sounded like she didn't want to admit it, but Avery wasn't much of a liar, either. "Kind of a grouchy crankypants, but a good man."

"How am I supposed to know what's real and what's a lie? I can't trust him." She couldn't trust the peace she'd felt *because* of him. No matter how much she wanted to.

"Honey, he told you his real name, and I doubt he bothered to come up with an entire fictional backstory. If I had my guess, it sounds like the only thing he didn't tell you was why he was in Europe to begin with."

"You can't know that. He... He said all the right things to make me think I was doing this. He played me."

"I don't know about that. But *you* do. One way or another, you have to trust your instincts."

"I don't have any instincts left." Every step she'd made along the way was the wrong one, from what she chose to major in to whom she almost married. It was all wrong.

Avery sighed. "Yeah, you do. You've just been such a

people pleaser since Mom died that you buried them deep. Why don't you take a few days, see some stuff, and figure out how you feel? If you want to tell Jacks to take a flying leap after that, do it. If you want to give him another chance, well, that's an option, too. It's your choice."

Her choice. She felt like she'd spent so much of the last ten years just reacting. Booking the ticket to Cork was the first time she'd been proactive in her own life, and look where it had led her—in Venice alone, nursing a broken heart. "I'm afraid."

She laughed. "You jumped on a plane to Europe with no plan. That's as brave as a person gets. Just trust yourself."

Her chest felt too tight. Did Avery know how hard it'd be for her to take that leap of faith where he was concerned? Every time she'd done it in the past, she'd been kicked in the face as a result. No matter what her sister thought, she couldn't argue with Alexis's track record. Who was to say her time with Luke was any different?

But…it had *felt* different. She'd never responded to Eric—or anyone else—the way she did with Luke. He'd brought out a side of her she didn't know existed, a strong and snappy woman she'd been certain was broken a long time ago. Maybe Avery *did* know how difficult it'd be for her, but her sister wanted Alexis happy. She'd move heaven and earth to make it happen if it was within her power. Alexis fought back the tightness in her throat. "I love you."

"I love you, too. Now go sightsee or whatever. Take lots of pictures!"

"I will. I promise." She hung up, feeling marginally better. Trust her gut. Easier said than done, but at least she didn't have to make a decision now. She could see a few more things, eat some amazing food, and then figure out how she felt about Luke.

Alexis had the creeping sense that she already knew damn well how she felt about it. She just needed some time to come to terms with it.

Chapter Twenty

Three days. Three goddamn days with no word. Not that Luke really expected one, but he'd prowled around Venice until he was ready to go out of his mind. There was no reason to think Alexis would stay in the city after their blowout, but that didn't stop him from looking for her.

It also gave him a lot of time to think.

The kernel of realization that started during his conversation with that bartender, Tristina, bloomed into full-out self-loathing. If he'd been honest with Alexis from the beginning—Flannery be damned—then he could have avoided hurting her like this. The more he thought about it, the more he wondered if they wouldn't have progressed in a similar way even if she knew why he was in Europe to begin with. It wasn't like they'd been best friends from the start.

He could have experienced those same things with her without the layer of lies between them. He could have been next to her while she discovered her inner strength without hobbling her along the way.

Because he *had* been telling the truth. She stood on her own two feet, even when he wasn't completely honest with her. Watching that confidence crumble was almost worse than knowing he'd fucked this up beyond all reason.

Not to mention he had to call and report in—something he'd avoided up to this point, mostly because he didn't want to face Flannery's wrath. If the man didn't know what happened between them—and that was doubtful at this point—Luke hadn't wanted to be the one to tell him.

Which was cowardly as fuck.

If he couldn't deal with confronting Flannery, then how the hell was he supposed to prove to Alexis that he was serious about her? Steeling himself, Luke dropped onto the bed in his hotel room and dug out his satellite phone.

It barely rang once. "I wondered when I'd hear from you."

There was nothing in Flannery's voice to tell him which way the wind was blowing. But the lack of panic told him all he needed to know. "You've talked to her?" She was okay. That was all that mattered.

"You have some serious balls to call me and demand to know a damn thing about her. Why don't we talk about the fact that you abused the hell out of my instructions? What part of 'protect Alexis' translated into 'fuck her'?"

"Don't talk about her like that." He shoved to his feet and paced around the bed and back again. "I didn't plan on things playing out this way, but I'm not going to apologize for it. I care about her and, yeah, I fucked up, but I'm going to find a way to make this right. I'm not letting her go without a fight."

He expected Flannery to lay into him, or at least rip him a new one. But the man just hissed out a breath. "What makes you think she wants anything to do with you?"

"She probably doesn't. And if she tells me that after I pour out my heart"—did he actually just say that shit?—"then I won't bother her again. But I have to try. I can't let things stand as they are."

"You're serious."

"As a fucking heart attack. She got to me, man. I didn't mean for it to happen, but I'm a goner where she's concerned."

Another pause, longer this time. "Even if she decides to give you a second chance, that doesn't let you off the hook with me—or Avery and Drew."

He didn't give a flying fuck what they thought of him. Alexis was the only one who mattered. "Just tell me where she is. Give me a chance to at least try to fix this." He didn't have the first clue how he was supposed to do it, but he couldn't walk away now any more than he could before.

Then it hit him. He didn't need Flannery to tell him where she was going, because he already knew. "She's going to Verona, isn't she?" If she was feeling half the heartbreak he was at this point, she'd want that reassurance that love wasn't all a shit show. Hell, he'd like a little reassurance right now, too.

"Yeah." Flannery hesitated. "Good luck."

Luke hung up, his mind already on his destination. Verona. Juliet's Wall. He had to admit there was something that hit him right in the chest at the thought of never seeing her again. He wasn't the type to write love letters to a woman who would never receive them, but after the last few days, he understood the urge. At this point, he'd do that and more to make her sit still long enough to listen to what he had to say.

First, he needed a fucking train ticket.

Alexis sat on one of the benches in the little courtyard and stared at the wall peppered with more letters than she could begin to count. Thousands of lovers pouring out their hearts to Juliet. She wasn't sure if it was romantic or horribly sad. In her current mood, she leaned toward the latter.

Hadn't she learned the hard way that life was more than willing to pass you by if you sat back and waited for something good to come? That's all she'd been doing for the last fifteen years, letting life guide her and, as a result, pass her by. If she'd been more proactive—more willing to put aside other people's expectations of her—would she be happy now? Maybe she would have found a man who was actually worth her love and settled down. The cancer… That was no one's fault. It still would have come no matter what choices she made. But it didn't have to be the destroying factor it'd turned into. She'd let the loss of her ability to have children take away everything else good in her.

No more.

She wasn't willing to sit back and wait. How many of the people who wrote these letters felt the same hopeless abyss she currently had fighting for dominance inside her?

All she could focus on was her memories of Luke and the realization that he'd been right—the way she'd grown had little to do with him. Yes, he'd made her body come alive and maybe acted as a catalyst to channel her returning self-confidence, but she would have gotten there on her own.

And the things he'd said to her…

She wanted what he'd been promising. She wanted it a lot. More than that, she *deserved* a man who wouldn't look at her and see all the places she was lacking. Luke saw her faults, but he also saw things worth admiring—all the good, the bad, and the ugly—and he didn't think she was a giant disappointment.

He was right.

She could face that now, could step away from the constant weight of other people's expectations. Which left the question—if she wasn't living for other people's needs, what did *she* want?

The answer was easier than she would have guessed.

She wanted Luke. She wanted the bickering and the long, sweaty nights spent in his arms, and the soft moments when they both lowered their battered emotional walls.

"Darlin'…"

For half a heartbeat, she thought she was hallucinating, but then Alexis looked up…straight into the sea-green eyes she'd become so familiar with since Cork. Still, she could hardly believe it. "Luke?"

He went to his knees in front of her, his slight grimace the only indication of how much the move must have hurt his old injury. "I've been waiting for two days for you to walk into this courtyard, darlin'."

Two days? She opened her mouth, but he held up a hand. "Hear me out. Please. I'm sorry. Christ, Alexis, you have no idea how sorry. I never should have lied to you about why

I was here, but I swear to God, I never lied about anything except the Marines, and if you give me a chance, I'll never lie to you again." He slipped something out of his pocket and pressed it into her hand.

She frowned. "What's this?"

"You said Juliet's Wall was filled with letters written to lost loves." He held her gaze, never wavering. "So I figured it was only right that I bring one of my own."

She stared at the paper. It had been ripped out of some hotel stationery and folded several times. From the creases, she got the feeling that Luke had opened and refolded it repeatedly since he wrote it. *He wrote me a letter, a letter in a place meant for lost loves. Does that mean…?* "Luke—"

"It's for you, darlin'. It was always for you."

Hesitantly, she unfolded it, her heart in her throat as she read. It was short and to the point, just like Luke.

Alexis,

If I'm handing you this letter, chances are that I've already told you how badly I fucked up and how desperately I want to make it right. But I'll say it again. You're the first woman who's looked at me and seen that the man is more than the scars of his past. You didn't flinch. You didn't turn away. You just accepted it all and turned it into something to be proud of. You humble me, darlin'. Being around you makes me want to believe in fairy tales and true love, and gives me the strength to want to face my past and my fears—everything you've done since you got off that plane in Cork. I don't deserve you. But if you give me a chance to make things right, I'll spend the rest of my life working to be a man worthy of you.

I love you, darlin'.

Feelings welled up inside her, nearly too much to contain. He'd come for her. More than that, the words he'd written seemed aimed for her very soul. This wasn't a lie. It was too raw and vulnerable to be fake. Her hands shook as that truth rolled over her. *It's real. It's all been real.* "You… love me?"

"I do." His frown deepened. "I know the letter isn't much, but—"

"Stop." She took his hands and urged him up onto the bench next to her. "The letter is perfect. It's everything. I…" There was no denying the truth. Not now, not here, not with him looking at her with a fragile hope in his eyes. "I love you, too. And you weren't the only one who made mistakes. I never should have said some of those things to you. I'm sorry, too."

"I deserved every word out of your mouth." He started to reach for her, and visibly restrained himself. "I know it's going to take time to re-earn your trust, but I'm willing to do whatever it takes."

"Kiss me."

He blinked. "What?"

"Do you need a written invitation?" She grabbed the front of his shirt and pulled him closer. "Kiss me like you mean it, Luke Jackson."

"That's no hardship." But he leaned in slowly, as if doubting this was what she really wanted. Alexis hooked the back of his neck and towed him to her, nipping his bottom lip before she teased his mouth open.

This was perfection. Kissing Luke felt a whole lot like coming home. And then his arms were around her and he was pulling her into his lap, and she knew without a doubt that she'd found exactly what she'd come to Europe looking for.

She pulled away. "Come home with me."

"Only if you promise to come down to Mississippi afterward. My auntie will be wanting to meet the woman who stole my heart." He grinned, making her heart skip a beat. "But there's time. I plan on spending the rest of my life with you, darlin', so if you want to pick up and go see the world, I'm there every step of the way. I'll always be there."

Epilogue

Luke touched his pocket for the seventeenth time in the last hour. He knew he was being crazy, but he couldn't seem to stop. Things were going too damn well—they had been for the last six months. After he and Alexis came back from Europe, there was some hashing out to do with the Flannery brothers and Avery, but it had fallen out okay when all was said and done.

Really, he would have gone through that and worse if it meant Alexis would be by his side at the end of it.

He reached over and took her hand, earning an absent-minded smile before she went back to baby-talking at her nephew, Braeden. In the kitchen, her sister was working up some kind of magic for dinner and chatting happily with Drew Flannery. It was the very epitome of domestic bliss.

He never thought he'd make it here. Not in a thousand years. And yet here he was, surrounded by Alexis's family—minus her grandparents—and creating a life for himself up here alongside her.

She'd fit in just as well down in Mississippi. As expected, Aunt Rose took to her like a pig in mud. Alexis might have been happy settling down there if not for the fact that her sister, father, and nephew were up in Pennsylvania. They hadn't officially picked a place, but he wouldn't be the one to ask her to leave them behind, especially now that she'd managed to acquire a modicum of peace here in Wellingford.

"Luke?"

He startled, and glanced up to find Alexis's dad, Sheng, watching him. From the look on his face, he must have been trying to get his attention for a few minutes. "Sorry?"

Sheng smiled. "I asked if you'd mind helping me bring in the groceries from my car?"

"Oh. Yeah. Sure." It was the perfect opportunity. He'd been wondering how the hell he was going to get Alexis's dad alone, and here the man was, offering him the chance on a silver platter. Luke followed him out the front door and down the walkway to where the cars were parked.

Sheng opened his trunk and turned to face him. "I believe you have something you want to ask me."

Luke blinked. "What?" His hand went to his pocket before he caught himself.

"Either you've been hiding the fact that you're a smoker for the last six months and are craving a cigarette, or there's a ring in your pocket." Sheng eyed him. "A ring with my oldest daughter's name on it."

He should have known the other man would pick up on his fidgeting. If he'd learned anything in the past six months, it was that not much got past Alexis's father. How the man put up with his own parents was a mystery to Luke, since they were the most unbearable people he'd ever had the displeasure of meeting. He cleared his throat. "I love your daughter. We didn't get off to the easiest of starts, but when's all said and done, I'd walk through hell and back for her if she asked me to. The only future that matters is the one I share with her—if she'll have me."

Here was the hard part. He didn't really want to put everything on Sheng's blessing, but it would mean a lot to both his potential future father-in-law and Alexis if he did. So, for her, he was jumping through this particular hoop. "I'd like your blessing before I ask her to marry me."

Sheng watched him for so long, it was a fight not to squirm. "My daughters mean very much to me, Luke. The world. I've had the pleasure of seeing Avery make her way in the world and carve out her happiness. Alexis hasn't had the same choices available to her."

Meaning she couldn't have kids. "I care about her—not some mythical future with a white picket fence and a few kids." He'd been as broken as Alexis when they first met—more so in a lot of ways. They might have started on their respective paths to redemption separately, but together they'd fought their way back into the light. Nothing else mattered compared to that.

Sheng nodded as if he'd said more than he realized. "You aren't the one I would have chosen for her." He held up his hand before Luke had a chance to cut in. "But I would have been wrong. My daughter lights up when you walk into the room. That alone would have been enough to give you my blessing. But Alexis is a grown woman and more than capable of choosing the man she wants to marry. If my daughter will have you, I'd be proud to call you my son-in-law." He nodded at the front door. "I think now's a good time to ask."

Luke turned to find Alexis standing on the porch, a small frown on her face. "This looks like an awfully serious conversation for coming out here to haul in some beer."

"I didn't need as much help as I thought." Sheng grabbed two plastic bags and a case of some kind of microbrew Luke had never heard of and strode into the house.

She frowned harder. "What was all that about? I think it's a little late for Dad to be warning you off, but then, he didn't have much of a chance to do that kind of thing in high school." Abruptly her frown disappeared and she grinned. "Did he threaten to bring out his shotgun? If it makes you feel any better, I'm pretty sure he doesn't even own one."

"Get over here." He held out his hand, secretly delighted when she didn't hesitate to come down the porch stairs and into his arms. He never stopped being amazed that this woman was his. Some days it all felt like a fever dream, and then he'd roll over and there she'd be, in his bed and his life and his heart. He wanted that forever. "I love you."

"I love you, too. But now you're starting to worry me."

It was now or never. He'd thought about doing this in front of her whole family, but this felt right. This thing between them had started in another country with only the two of them. It was right that the next step should happen without an audience present.

He went down on one knee, ignoring the twinge the move caused. "Alexis Yeung, it's been a hell of a six months. We've backpacked across Europe. I've met your family and managed to survive to tell the tale. My auntie is ready to adopt you if I don't pull my head out of my ass and make an honest woman of you—that's a direct quote in case you were wondering." He reached into his pocket and pulled out the ring case. "But at the end of the day, the only thing that matters is that you are the single most amazing woman I've ever met. You humble me on a daily basis with your strength, and you inspire me to be a better man. I love waking up next to you, and I want to spend the rest of our lives conquering whatever challenges life decides to throw at us, whether it's climbing a cliff to face your worst fear or kicking some sense into me when I need it most. So, Alexis Yeung, will you do me the honor of becoming my wife?"

Her eyes were wide, and her hand in his shook. "Marriage?"

"If you'll have me." He couldn't read the expression on her face, and it made him nervous.

"But Luke, I can't have kids. We can't—"

"Do you want kids?"

She blinked. "What?"

"It's a simple enough question. Do you want kids? Because if you don't, I'm down with that. If you do, there's always adoption." He squeezed her hand. "I don't care about bloodlines, darlin'. If we adopt, the kid that we choose is going to be *our* kid, and I'll knock anyone who says otherwise in the dirt."

She snorted. "You can't just go around beating up anyone who says something you don't like."

"Watch me." He opened the ring box and turned it to face her. The ring was a one-and-a-half-carat princess-cut diamond. It was in a simple setting, but it was elegant in its simplicity. "What do you say?"

"As if there was any question." She grinned, her eyes shining. "Yes, Luke Jackson, I want to be your wife and adopt babies with you and spend the rest of my life by your side."

"Well hell, darlin', you had me worried there for a second." He slipped the ring onto her finger and pushed to his feet. "That was mighty mean of you to drag it out like that."

"A little nerves never hurt anyone." She went up onto her tiptoes and kissed him. "I love you so freaking much. I still can't believe that things are so crazy perfect."

He held her close. He'd do everything in his power to make his woman happy. *My woman. She said yes*. He spun her around, loving the way she laughed. "Then it's a good thing you have the rest of your life to get used to the idea."

About the Author

New York Times and *USA Today* bestselling author, Katee Robert, learned to tell stories at her grandpa's knee. Her favorites then were the rather epic adventures of The Three Bears, but at age twelve she discovered romance novels and never looked back. Though she dabbled in writing, life got in the way, as it often does, and she spent a few years traveling, living in both Philadelphia and Germany. In between traveling and raising her two wee ones, she had the crazy idea that she'd like to write a book and try to get published.

Discover the* Out of Uniform *series…

IN BED WITH MR. WRONG

Air Force Pararescuer Ryan Flannery avoids his hometown at all costs, so he's not thrilled when he's set up on a blind date… until meets mousy librarian Brianne Nave. Her sweet curves and kissable lips are like a siren's call, but her smart mouth? Not so much. How can two people have so little chemistry outside the bedroom when they fit together so perfectly in it? Stranded in a cabin by their friends, they'll be forced to find out—if they don't kill each other first.

HIS TO KEEP

FALLING FOR HIS BEST FRIEND

Also by Katee Robert

COME UNDONE SERIES

WRONG BED, RIGHT GUY

CHASING MRS. RIGHT

TWO WRONGS, ONE RIGHT

SEDUCING MR. RIGHT

SERVE SERIES

MISTAKEN BY FATE

Betting on Fate

Protecting Fate

Seducing the Bridesmaid

Meeting His Match

Sanctify series

The High Priestess

Queen of Swords

Queen of Wands

CPSIA information can be obtained
at www.ICGtesting.com
Printed in the USA
LVHW092255160619
621424LV00001B/7/P